Designing Love

Designing Love

SUNRIVER DREAMS BOOK THREE

By Kimberly Rose Johnson

Designing Love
Published by Mountain Brook Ink
White Salmon, WA U.S.A.

The website addresses recommended throughout this book are offered as a resource. These websites are not intended in any way to be or imply an endorsement on the part of Mountain Brook Ink, nor do we vouch for their content.

This story is a work of fiction. All characters and events are the product of the author's imagination. Any resemblance to any person, living or dead, is coincidental.

Scripture quotations are taken from the King James Version of the Bible. Public domain.
ISBN 978-1-943959-22-8

The Team: Miralee Ferrell, Nikki Wright, Cindy Jackson
Cover Design: Indie Cover Design, Lynnette Bonner Designer

Mountain Brook Ink is an inspirational publisher offering fiction you can believe in.

Printed in the United States of America

To my dad. Thanks for showing such an interest in my writing and suggesting I use bible prophecy in this story.

Acknowledgements

I would like to thank everyone who had a hand in preparing this book for publication. Each and every one of you are invaluable, and I appreciate what you do. Thank you!

CHAPTER ONE

SIERRA ROBBINS SAT IN HER SUV outside a stone-faced mansion in Sunriver. This was the last place she ever expected to live. But the timing couldn't be more perfect.

"Whoa! You're housesitting *here*?" her fifteen-year-old son asked.

She looked over at Trey and grinned. "Yes, and I expect you to treat this place like a museum. Don't touch anything."

He laughed. "Not likely, but I get it. I'll be careful not to break anything." He opened his door and stepped out. "What're you waiting for? Don't you want to see inside?"

"I've been inside. Remember? Mrs. Drake was a client." Unease gripped her. Not for the first time anxiety settled on her as she grabbed her purse. Did she make a mistake agreeing to housesit? She took in the enormous house and pushed away her nervousness. There was no way living rent-free for a year could be a bad thing. They'd be living in luxury. Her son did online high school, so she didn't even need to worry about transporting him to and from Bend for school since Sunriver didn't have a public high school.

A man wearing a red flannel jacket walked around from the side of the house and waved. "You must be the Robbins'." He approached them and offered his hand. "Mrs. Drake said you'd be moving in today."

Sierra eyed the middle-aged looking man with a medium build and salt-and-pepper hair. "Yes. I'm sorry, but she didn't mention you."

He chuckled. "I suppose she wouldn't. I'm Carl." He pulled off a work glove and offered his hand. "I supply wood for the fireplace. These spring evenings and mornings can get pretty cold, so if you need to start a fire you'll find a good supply of wood in the garage."

Relief washed over her. "How thoughtful of Mrs. Drake. Thank you."

"Sure thing. If you need anything while you're here give me a call. I left my number taped to the door in the garage." Carl nodded to her son then wandered back in the direction he'd come from.

Odd. Why was he going across the landscape? He wove past junipers and a small boulder. Maybe he'd parked his truck on that side of the property, but still kind of peculiar. She shook off the strange encounter as she pulled a key from her purse and marched up the wide concrete stairs leading to the front door. Trey took the stairs two at a time and stood waiting at the top for her. She tossed him the keys. "Remember don't touch *anything*! The art alone in this house could fund your college education."

Sierra stood in the grand entrance that opened onto a great room with a connected kitchen and dining room to the left and a hall to the bedrooms on the right of the great room. The cool color scheme wasn't her favorite, but the home could easily grace the cover of a magazine. The heels of her boots clicked across the hardwood flooring as she made her way to the far wall of windows that faced Mount Bachelor. She opened the drapes and caught her breath.

Although the ponderosa pines obscured the view, it really was breathtaking. It would be difficult to leave this house next spring.

"This place is amazing. Can I pick any room?" he asked as he wandered from one room into another.

"No. Mrs. Drake specifically said you should stay in the first floor guestroom off the entrance."

He popped his head around a corner. "Oh. Okay. I'll get our bags." Trey breezed outside, and a moment later shouts filled the air.

She ran to the door and froze. A police officer had his gun drawn on Trey who lay face down on the paved driveway. "What are you doing?" she shouted trying to keep her voice calm, but clearly failing.

He jerked his head toward her. "You're trespassing."

"No, we're not. I'm Sierra Robbins. Mrs. Drake told the security company that my son and I would be living here for the next twelve months."

He spoke into the radio on his shoulder, still keeping an eye on her with his gun leveled at her son.

Time ticked slowly as she waited for him to confirm her story. "You don't need to point that thing at him. He's not going to hurt you." She heard a muddled voice coming from his radio.

"Sorry about that, ma'am." He lowered his weapon and holstered it. "You can get up now."

Trey stood. His face had turned ash white, and he visibly shook as he glared at the cop.

Sierra rushed down the stairs on wobbly legs to her son's side, swallowing back overwhelming emotion. She took a deep breath then let it out slowly as she placed a hand on Trey's shoulder. She'd love to wrap him in her arms, but he stood over a foot taller than she did and didn't like public displays of affection.

"I'm Officer Spencer Preston." He offered his hand.

She took it, though begrudgingly. "This is my son, Trey." Where did he get off pointing a gun at her son one minute, then shaking her hand the next? But she didn't want trouble, so she kept her thoughts to herself.

"You triggered the silent alarm."

Sierra's heart skittered. "That's right. I forgot. Mrs. Drake told me I would need to disarm it. I'm so sorry, officer." She offered the stocky blond man a tentative smile, wishing he'd leave. "I have the owner's phone number memorized. If you call her, she will clear this whole matter up."

"No need. Everything is fine now."

"Good. You sure got here fast."

"I was nearby when the call came in. Are you and your son new to Sunriver?"

"In a way. I work for a local interior design company, but before this we lived in Bend."

He nodded. "Welcome to the neighborhood. Most of the homes on this street are rentals." He pointed to one three doors down and across the street. "Your closest full-time neighbor lives there. A retired couple."

"You seem to be well acquainted with this area."

He raised his chin. "I try to make sure I know as many of the locals as possible."

"Does this mean you come around a lot?" her son asked with a hint of annoyance in his voice.

She couldn't blame him, but she didn't allow sass. "Trey." The warning was all it took.

"Sorry. Excuse me." He marched past them and

opened the back of the SUV.

Officer Preston frowned. "I suppose I made a bad first impression on him. I'm sorry about that."

"It was an honest mistake and my own fault. I should have remembered to turn off the alarm. I guess Carl must have reset it when he left. Strange too since he knew I was here."

"Carl?" The officer asked.

"Yes. The man who was here when we arrived. Apparently he delivers firewood."

Spencer frowned. "Maybe *he* triggered the alarm."

She shook her head. "No. He knew who I was and that Mrs. Drake was expecting me."

"I see." He looked around as if looking for something or someone. "Will your husband be joining you, too?"

She narrowed her eyes. "Why do you ask?"

"Just like to know who is supposed to be here and who isn't." He raised a brow.

Irritation surged through her. This dude was seriously getting on her nerves. He didn't need to know her personal business. "No one else will be joining us. Please excuse me." She walked over to her SUV and stacked one box onto another before hoisting them into her arms. She strutted by the cop who stood there for a moment before going to the police SUV and driving off. Whew!

Spencer Preston stood at the water cooler in the bullpen at the police station unable to get the pretty blonde who hadn't been wearing a wedding ring off his mind.

"Hey, Spencer. How'd it go today?" Mark, his buddy and fellow officer, asked.

"Fine."

Mark crossed his arms and narrowed his eyes. "You are too easy to read. What happened?"

"Nothing."

Mark motioned for him to follow him into the conference room. "What's going on?"

Spencer ran a hand along the back of his neck. "I responded to a silent alarm call today. It turned out to be the house sitter who forgot there was an alarm."

"And?"

Mark knew him too well. "And nothing." He didn't do anything wrong, but he couldn't shake that what happened today would be life altering.

"Nope." Mark shook his head. "I'm not buying what you're selling. Tell me."

"The woman intrigued me."

"How so? Is she someone we need to keep an eye on?"

"No. Nothing like that. I mean she snagged my interest." Except for one problem—her son. There was no way the teen would ever let go of what happened.

His buddy grinned. "Caught your eye, huh? I was beginning to think you were destined to remain single forever."

Spencer playfully slugged him in the gut. "Watch it. You've been here all of ten months. You don't know everything about me." Nor would he. There were some things he didn't talk about. Even with a good friend like Mark.

"Good point. Sorry. Catch you later." Mark sauntered to his desk and sat facing his computer.

Spencer was glad Mark didn't know his past. He would likely only judge him. He'd judged himself enough and didn't need any help knowing what a fool he'd been. He waved to whoever might be paying attention as he left for the evening. It'd been a long day, and he was ready for the peace and quiet of his little house, situated on the south side of Sunriver. It wasn't grand or glamorous, but it was affordable and close to work.

An image of the woman from the silent-alarm house flashed in his mind as he climbed into his pickup. Her fear-filled eyes heaped a load of guilt on him. He hated that he'd frightened Ms. Robbins and her son. She didn't look old enough to have a teenager. But he was smart enough to know people didn't always look their age, and some women had kids when they were young. Which one was she?

A sudden idea hit him, and with renewed energy he headed to the Sunriver Village. He found exactly what he was looking for at the grocery store and purchased it. Who didn't love chocolate cake?

A short time later, he pulled into the driveway of the house he'd been called to this afternoon, grabbed the cake, and got out. "Here goes nothing." The street looked as quiet as he'd expected. It wouldn't get busy until the weekend when tourists flocked to the resort community in droves to play in this Central Oregon playground.

He marched up the steps and rang the doorbell that gonged and seemed to echo. A moment later Sierra pulled the door open. "Officer Preston?"

He held out the chocolate cake. "I brought a peace offering. I felt bad about earlier, even if I was doing my job. That's no way to be welcomed to the neighborhood."

She hesitantly took the cake. "Thank you."

"Who is it, Mom?" Her son came up behind her and scowled when he spotted Spencer.

"Just your local police officer bringing a welcome-to-the-neighborhood cake." Spencer quirked a grin. Talk about corny. This had been a bad idea—one of his worst.

The kid frowned. Not the response he was hoping for.

Sierra stepped aside. "Trey, what do you say to Officer Preston?"

"Call me Spencer."

Trey's eyes narrowed. "Thanks, Spencer. For the record, my mom doesn't date."

"Trey!" Sierra's face reddened.

The teen shrugged. "What? You don't. And we both know he's only here because he either feels like a jerk for pulling a gun on me or he's interested in you."

"That's enough."

Apparently Trey had a little sense in his head, considering he took the cake and darted away.

"I apologize for my son. I'm afraid what happened this afternoon has had a lasting effect. He might need a few days . . . or months to get over it."

"I'm really sorry to hear that. I had no way of knowing you and your son weren't burglarizing the place. I wouldn't have been doing my job if I hadn't stopped him."

"Good point."

Spencer nodded.

A car pulled up behind his, and Bailey Calderwood got out. "Hey there, Spencer. What's going on? I didn't realize you knew Sierra." She strode up the stairs and stopped beside him.

He gave her the shortened version of what had happened and why he was there.

She shot a worried look at Sierra. "Are you okay?"

"I'm fine. What brings you by?"

"I wanted to see how your move went and if you needed anything."

"For the most part everything went well. That was really nice of you to stop in to check on us."

"I also brought you this." Bailey opened her purse and pulled out a paint wheel. "I've marked the colors I need you to order." She then removed two squares of fabric. "The homeowner decided to go with custom drapes and sheers. I'll leave that in your capable hands."

Spencer stood there silently taking in the women's conversation. Bailey was a friend of a friend. She managed the design side of Belafonte Construction and Design, a local interior decorating company that worked alongside the other branch of the company—new home construction and remodeling. So Sierra must be the assistant he'd heard so much about. He should've put that together this afternoon when she said she worked for an interior design company.

"Do you want a slice, Spencer?" Sierra asked.

Both women stood there looking at him like he was a miscreant child.

"Why are you looking at me like I stole cookies from the cookie jar? What'd I miss?"

They both grinned and said in unison, "Nothing."

He took a step back. "O-kay. I'll be headed home then. Have a good evening, and I hope you enjoy the cake."

"We will," Bailey called after him as he retreated to his pickup.

He raised a hand and quickly got inside his pickup. He knew better than to daydream in the presence of two women. Too bad Bailey had stopped by. He'd really hoped to clear the air between himself, Sierra, and Trey.

He'd have to find another way to make this afternoon up to them. But how?

CHAPTER TWO

SIERRA SAT ACROSS THE DINING room table from her boss with Trey between them.

Trey shoveled the cake into his mouth.

"Take it easy. I don't want you to choke." Sierra stood and filled a glass with water then placed it before her son.

He swallowed then guzzled the water. "Thanks. That was good. What's for dinner?"

Bailey laughed. "You didn't feed your son dinner before dessert?"

"Well, I wasn't expecting a cake delivery." She nodded to Trey. "How about you call in a pizza, and I'll go pick it up?"

"Score! Pizza *and* cake. You'd think it was someone's birthday." Trey grinned for the first time since the incident with the police officer earlier.

"After the day we've had, you deserve it. Officer Preston brought the cake by to make amends. I hope you'll forgive him."

Trey frowned. "He doesn't deserve it."

"It was an honest mistake, and I'm just as much to blame for not turning off the alarm."

"Whatever." He pushed back his chair and stood. "I'll be in my room."

Sierra sighed.

"What was that all about?

She told her boss the full story, filling in the blanks Spencer had left out earlier.

"Whoa. I'm sorry Trey went through that. But Spencer is a good guy and a good cop too. He works with Nicole's husband, and Nicole only has good things to say about him. In fact, I probably should have talked with him about something that happened at the site Rick is working on."

"What are you talking about?" Her mind darted to Rick, the oldest Belafonte brother who headed up all the construction jobs.

"It's not really a big deal. Some equipment appeared to be pushed over. Weird things have been happening off and on for a while now. Back in November vandals spray-painted cabinets inside a new build near Bend. Rick says vandalism every now and then is normal, but I have a funny feeling."

"Like what?"

"I'm not sure. It feels like more than a prank to me."

"Hmm. Toppling equipment is kind of weird, isn't it?" Sierra asked.

"I think so. Thankfully nothing was damaged, other than a gauge, which can be fixed. Nicole's husband Mark responded when Rick called the police. If he's on the case I know this will get resolved soon. He's a great detective."

Sierra nodded. Bailey and Nicole were best friends, and she and Stephen often socialized with Nicole and her husband. Bailey and Stephen had been dating practically since Sierra had started as her assistant around Christmas, and unless she was wrong, the CEO of Belafonte Designs would soon be popping the question. Would that put her out of a job? She could see the two of them working closely together once they were married. From what Sierra had observed, Stephen had an eye for interior design as much or more than she did—but his main job was drawing up house plans. Maybe her position was safe after all. Not that Bailey ever gave her much free reign to show what she could do. Her job consisted of more grunt work than anything. She probably didn't need to worry.

"What's wrong?" Bailey asked with concern in her eyes.

"Nothing really. Other than I'm concerned about Trey. The incident this afternoon really messed with his head."

"I'd think it would have that effect on most people. It's not every day a cop orders you to the ground and holds a gun on you."

"Praise the Lord for that." She stood. "I'd better order pizza. Would you like to stay and join us, or do you and Stephen have dinner plans?"

"I'm solo tonight. I'd love to stick around if you don't mind."

"Not at all." She liked her boss, although they never socialized, so this felt a little weird. Maybe Bailey was concerned about the whole thing with Spencer. But it wasn't necessary. They were going to be fine . . . eventually. Sierra grabbed her cellphone, and placed the order for an extra large Canadian bacon and pineapple pizza.

"I know we're off the clock, but are you enjoying your job?" Bailey asked.

"Mostly. I was hoping to be able to make more design decisions."

Empathy filled Bailey's eyes. "Yes. And I hope that will change soon. In fact, John, Stephen's middle brother, asked to have a more hands on role in the company—as in he'd like to get out of the office and work some jobs. If things pick up, I plan to have the two of you work together."

"Really?" Her pulse picked up. She'd never formally met John, but the man made her heart flutter when they'd spoken on the phone. There was something about his voice. "But doesn't he run the business side of things?"

"Yes, and I'm honestly not sure how it will work, but Rick and Stephen are willing to give it a try."

"Hmm. Interesting. So I'd be paired with him." She winced at how that sounded. "I don't mean as a couple." Although she wouldn't mind. What was she thinking? She couldn't afford to get involved with anyone. Trey spoke the truth—she didn't date and for good reason. She would never allow another man into their lives so he could abandon them when things got tough. She'd much rather be alone than go through that again.

Bailey chuckled. "I didn't think you did. Are you okay about working with John? You seem hesitant."

"No. I'm surprised that's all."

"Me too." Bailey stared at the screen on her phone and started typing. "I'm sorry, Sierra, but I need to go. I forgot I promised to take care of Lacy and Collin tonight." She stood and shouldered her oversized purse. "Thanks for the cake."

"Sure thing. Have fun."

"We will. I'll see myself out." Bailey raced to the door and closed it softly behind her.

Bailey's boyfriend's niece and nephew seemed to always need a sitter. She almost felt sorry for them, but they appeared to be happy and healthy children. She shrugged. It was none of her business, and she had enough trouble of her own without pondering her boss. What would John be like to work with? Granted there was only an off chance they'd work together. She'd been with the company for several months now, and although they were always busy, it was never more than they could handle. But maybe that was by design.

Sierra strode through the great room and into the hall. She stopped in Trey's doorway. "You want to come along or stay here?"

"Can I drive?"

"Sure." She tossed him the keys. It made her nervous to drive with him in Bend, but Sunriver, with its single lane roads in each direction were a piece of cake, even for a young driver with only a permit. Besides, it'd give him more experience with the traffic circles that were so prevalent here and in certain areas of Bend.

Thirty minutes later, they were home with their pizza sitting at the dining room table once again.

"This is good. I think I'm going to like living in Sunriver if we get pizza at least once a week." He shot her a teasing grin.

"Mmm-hmm. We'll see about that." Although taking a night off from cooking once a week sounded great. "Do you like this house?"

"What's not to like?"

"Good. Then you won't mind your chores."

He stopped chewing, and his face went slack.

"As long as we're on unpleasant topics, how is your college search coming along?"

He chuckled. "It's only unpleasant for you, Mom. I think it's fun. I can't wait until I graduate and head off to school."

"You have a couple of years to go, so don't get too excited." She should be happy her son was almost ready for adulthood and excited about college. A part of her wanted to keep him with her indefinitely, but that would not be good for either of them in the grand scheme of life.

"I know, but I need to start narrowing down my choices so I can visit the campuses of my top three."

"Is that what your teacher recommended?" Part of the curriculum for one of his online classes was to search out colleges that had the degree program he was interested in. She'd love to suggest he stay home and continue school online, but Trey needed the college experience. Traditional high school hadn't worked for him, but they both had high hopes he'd find a good fit for college.

"Yeah. Think fast." He tossed a paper napkin at her.

She grabbed it midair and flicked it back at him.

"How do you do that every time? You never miss!"

"It's a gift." She stood and gathered their plates and dropped everything into the empty pizza box. "I'll do clean up tonight."

"Of course. Pick the easy night."

She chuckled, enjoying their easy banter. She'd devoted her life to raising her son. When she was sixteen and pregnant, she had considered giving him up for adoption because she wanted to finish high school and didn't know how she'd be able to take care of him, but her boyfriend wanted "the baby," as he always called him. Unfortunately, her boyfriend had a short attention span and abandoned them a year after Trey was born.

She'd managed to finish high school while working part time and raising her son with the help of friends and their parents, but it had been a struggle she wouldn't wish on anyone. Her own parents had kicked her out when she'd needed them the most. She never wanted to be like them and determined to always be there for Trey, even if that meant she lived alone for the rest of his growing-up years. She didn't trust a man to stick around and refused to put Trey through the kind of pain she'd experienced.

So much had changed over the past fifteen years. Although it took her longer than the average student, she had earned a Bachelor of Arts degree in interior design, and she was proud of her accomplishments. Granted she'd been unable to go into business for herself like she'd planned due to financial issues. Then she hadn't been able to find a job as an actual designer; but now that she'd landed a job as Bailey's assistant, she had confidence things would begin to fall into place. At least she hoped so, because Trey would be going off to college in a couple of years. She didn't want him to have to work his way through college like she had done or accumulate a large debt. No, she hoped and prayed she'd finally have a higher-paying job with enough money saved to get him a quality education. Housesitting for the next year would put her well on track to reach that goal since they were living here for free. Talk about a blessing. She didn't seek out the job, but when Mrs. Drake asked she couldn't say no.

"Mom?"

"Hmm." She glanced over her shoulder as she wiped the table.

"I want to meet my dad."

She sucked in a breath, closed her eyes and sat in the nearest chair. She had feared this day would come. She'd hoped since Trey hadn't mentioned it when he was young that maybe he never would. Now what? She had no idea where Randy was. When he walked out on them, he'd never looked back. His family had left town as well. Randy's parents had not been into being grandparents.

"Say something."

"Sorry. You really surprised me." She patted the chair beside her. "Come sit."

He did as she asked and turned expectant eyes on her.

"Why the sudden interest?"

Trey shrugged. "I'm not a kid anymore. I thought he might like me now," he mumbled. "I don't know. I just want to meet him."

Her son clearly held something back, but she didn't dare push him. He'd tell her his reasons when he was ready. At least she hoped he would. "Honey, your dad was eighteen when he and his family left. Not much older than you are now. He was too immature to be a dad. I didn't realize you believed he didn't like you." They should have had this talk years ago. Her throat thickened. How could her son think his dad didn't like him?

"You haven't denied it."

"I know deep down he loved you very much, but he didn't know what to do with a baby. It wasn't personal with you. He wasn't ready to be an adult."

His face changed to a pained look of disbelief. He shot up. "I'm going for a run."

"It's dark."

Ignoring her, he darted out the door.

She groaned and buried her face in her hands. *It wasn't personal?* How could she have said something so stupid? It was very personal. Should she go after Trey or let him cool off? She'd never catch him, considering the last time she ran was in a required college PE class. Every mom instinct in her said he needed her, but this time she had to let him be. He wasn't the kind of kid to get into trouble; however, today had been one of those life-altering kind of days.

An hour later Trey slunk into the house. His sweaty T-shirt clung to his lean body.

Sierra blinked back tears of relief. "Are you okay?"

He nodded and strode to the guest bathroom. A moment later the sound of running water filled the silent tomb of a house.

One way or another, she needed to locate Randy. He may not have wanted to be a dad at eighteen, but if her son had his way, things were about to change.

CHAPTER THREE

JOHN BELAFONTE HIT THE END BUTTON on his phone. Another messed up order. What was going on? Someone claiming to be his mother had changed a wallpaper order and shorted them three rolls. But Mom wouldn't do that, would she? He needed to have a talk with her in person to be certain. At least today was Friday, and he could spend the weekend far from the confines of these four walls after dealing with this latest issue.

For years he'd been happy taking care of the business side of the family company, but lately he'd grown discontent. Maybe it had to do with his mother's failing health, or maybe it was simply time for something new. Whatever the reason, he needed a change before he burned out and didn't want anything to do with Belafonte Construction and Design.

The door to the office swung open and Stephen stepped inside. "Hey there. Rick said he needed the work order for the house on Killdeer. I have a few free minutes, so thought I'd take care of it now."

"Right. He mentioned that when he called." John shuffled through the papers on his desk. His oldest brother rarely bothered to stop by the office since Stephen, his youngest brother, had returned home from an extended stay in France and had stepped in for Rick in some areas. "Here it is. Any more problems at the site?"

Stephen shook his head. "I heard about the wallpaper shortage. There's no way Mom did that."

"I don't think so either, but if she didn't, who did?" John thumbed through a stack of papers.

"I'm beginning to wonder about Sierra. Bailey thinks the world of her, but it's difficult to ignore the fact that things started happening around the time she was hired."

John rubbed his chin. "I've only spoken with her over the phone, but I never got any weird vibes that she was up to no good."

"Me neither, but I don't know what else to think."

"Let's not rush to judgment." John couldn't believe he was defending a woman he didn't know, but based on their phone conversations, she seemed like a nice lady. He couldn't picture her attempting to sabotage their company. But if not her, then who?

"I won't. Innocent until proven guilty is my mantra. Besides, I can't imagine her risking her job by going to one of our sites and trying to damage our equipment. Why would she do that? She has nothing to gain and everything to lose. I wonder if an animal got in there and knocked over the equipment."

"It's possible, but highly unlikely. Mark came by and suggested it was probably kids. There was no evidence that an animal had been in the house."

"Other than the two legged kind."

John shook his head. Kids had probably gotten into the house and thought it'd be fun to overturn their stuff. The phone rang. "Hold on a sec." He answered the business line and listened to the man on the other end. "Yes, sir. That's exactly the kind of work we do."

Stephen sat in an old leather chair that faced the desk

and tapped his fingers on the armrest.

"Yes. I can have someone stop by your place this evening." He talked with the man a little longer then hung up. "Yes!"

Stephen chuckled. "What's going on?"

"We don't have the job yet, but we *need* this one." Need was relative—he wanted it. The busier they were, the greater chance he had of stepping out of this office and getting his hands dirty. He needed a change.

He wrote the address on a sticky note and handed it to his brother. "They want a huge remodel. Can you and Bailey go by there this evening at six to meet with the homeowners?"

"Tonight? Let me check with her." Stephen sent a text and waited.

John watched his brother's lips tip up and fought the surprising bout of jealousy that arose. Stephen had been dating Bailey since Christmas, and although they'd only been together a few months, he could tell they were serious. He was happy for Stephen; his brother's first wife had died of melanoma about three years ago, and he deserved to find love again. He only wished to find love for himself, too.

If only John's life could be so blessed.

"Bailey said no problem."

"Great." John went on to explain what the potential client wanted. "Call me after you meet with them. I want to know how it went."

"Will do." Stephen stood. "You okay?"

He nodded. They'd grown closer since Stephen's return from France, but he wasn't ready to discuss where his head was. "I'll talk to you later."

"Okay." Stephen waved then headed outside.

The quiet swirled around him, almost choking him. Suddenly the office was a prison again. He needed to get out, even if it was only ten in the morning! He programed the business line to forward to his cell then locked up. Early or not, a change in scenery was in order. Now.

About thirty minutes later he pulled up to his mother's house and put his rig in park. Mom had suffered a stroke around eight months ago, and she had never fully recovered. It was a miracle she was still living, all things considered. He almost felt silly coming by to see if she had called their vendor, but he needed to rule his mother out. He rarely stopped by during work hours, but there was no rule stating she could only have visitors in the evening. He whistled a favorite worship song as he strode to the door. He rapped on the door then poked his head inside. "Anyone home?"

Heels tapped across the hardwood flooring as Bailey walked toward him from the direction of the kitchen. "Hi, John. Did you need something?"

He saw the confusion on her face. "I thought I'd stop in and see my mom." There was no reason she needed to know why he wanted to visit his mother.

"Oh. I'm sorry. Stephen took her to a doctor's appointment."

His shoulders slumped. "Seriously? He was just in the Bend office a little while ago." He should have said something to Stephen about coming here to see their mom.

"He probably took Mona to her appointment then swung over to the office while he waited. I'm sorry you missed her. She's been doing a little better lately. She'll be disappointed to have missed you."

"I should have called first."

"It's fine. I hear we have a potential new client. I'm looking forward to meeting with them this evening."

"Bailey." A petite blonde stepped from the home office with her face buried in a wallpaper catalogue. "I think I found the perfect paper for the bedroom." She looked up and stopped short. "Oh. Sorry. I didn't realize anyone was here. Hi, John."

"Sierra, right?" He recognized Bailey's assistant's voice from their phone conversations. "You know my name?"

Her cheeks pinked ever so slightly. "Well, your picture is on the wall along with your brothers' in the office. I've met Rick and Stephen, so you have to be John."

"In the flesh." He grinned. She was as cute in person as she'd sounded on the phone. There was no way she could be the person sabotaging their company—could she? She had the brains to come up with a scheme, but Bailey spoke highly of her. Still, he couldn't figure how she could benefit from harassing the company she worked for.

"I'll be in the office," she said to Bailey then spared him another glance.

"Thanks, Sierra," Bailey said. "I'll join you shortly."

"I didn't mean to scare her away." He hoped the opposite—he wouldn't mind having missed his mother if he could get to know Sierra a little. It would be nice to be able to confirm his belief that she was innocent. He'd been charmed when they'd spoken on the phone, and now that he'd seen her, he was more so.

She chuckled. "You didn't. She's focused when she's working."

He nodded. "When do you expect my mom and

brother to be back?"

"I have no idea. If the doctor is on time then within the hour, if not . . ." She shrugged. "Oh, and Stephen mentioned taking her out to eat too, so it's anyone's guess when they'll be back."

"I see. Okay." Disappointed, he turned toward the door. Although a waste of a drive, he would try and make the best of it by visiting the bakery in the village for a donut, then circle back here. Maybe then Sierra would be free to talk. Hopefully Mom wouldn't be gone for hours.

"You can wait here, if you'd like."

"I don't want to get in the way."

"Trust me. This house is plenty big enough for the three of us." She grinned and walked toward the office. "If you can't find something to keep you occupied, I'm sure we can find a task for you."

"That sounds like a challenge." He didn't really need a donut.

She tossed a grin over her shoulder. He chuckled. Bailey had come into her own these past several months since taking over for his mother. The first couple of years she worked for his mom she'd been somewhat shy and reserved, but since she started dating Stephen she'd changed. She had an air of confidence about her that she'd lacked before, and she was more assertive now—in a good way.

It was nice to see this side of her. Especially since the old Bailey would not have been able to run the design branch of the company half as well without her newly found confidence. He had to hand it to his little brother. Stephen had seen the potential in her and stoked it to life. Now it was Bailey's turn to groom Sierra. Although older than Bailey by a few years, Sierra didn't seem to mind having a younger boss, which bode well for all of them. From what Stephen had told him, Bailey's assistant showed a lot of promise as a designer. The woman definitely piqued his interest—one way or another, he'd find a way to get to know her.

CHAPTER FOUR

SIERRA GRAPPLED WITH NERVES KNOWING JOHN waited in the kitchen for his mother. He'd left for a while and popped his head in when he'd come back to see if Mona was home. What was so important he would wait for an undetermined amount of time for his mother's return? Could be he wanted to simply visit her, but she sensed there was more to it than that. He was a busy man. Why not return this evening after work? She stood and stretched.

Bailey looked up from her computer screen. "Everything okay?"

"Yes. I'm thirsty and thought I'd get some water. Can I get you anything?"

"No, thanks. I'm leaving in five. Aren't you joining me?" Confusion covered Bailey's face.

"Of course. I'll only be a minute." Thanks to the distraction of John being in the house, she'd forgotten they had a delivery to sort through and a bedroom to put together at a client's home. It was a fun project—a child's bedroom.

"On second thought, how about you grab a couple water bottles from the fridge, and we'll take them with us?" Bailey stood and closed her laptop. "I'll meet you in the car."

"Will do." Disappointment struck Sierra as she

hustled to the kitchen. So much for finding out what was going on with John. She wasn't normally a busybody, but according to Bailey there was something different about him today—more serious. Not that she was looking for trouble, but if it had anything to do with Belafonte Designs, she wanted to know about it. This job was extremely important to her, and her son depended on her.

"Well, hello." John stood at the counter sipping from a mug. Coffee scented the air. He raised the mug. "Would you care for a cup? I could use the company. I'm feeling rather stupid for not thinking to call first to see if my mom was home before driving out here."

"Don't. Mona is almost always here. You had no way of knowing."

"Unless I'd called."

She grinned. "True."

"How about that coffee?" He pulled a cupboard open and reached inside.

"No time. Bailey and I are headed out." She grabbed two water bottles from the fridge. "Is everything okay? Although I assumed you stopped by to see your mother, I've never seen you here, so it seems odd." She turned and faced him.

A strained look covered his face. "I have something to talk to my mom about, and I prefer to do so in person."

"Okay. Well, I should go. Bailey is waiting." She fled the kitchen, grabbed her purse then rushed out to the car. She never should have questioned John. Clearly whatever the problem was, he had no intention of telling her, and to make matters worse, he seemed bothered by her inquiry. Rightly so, too. Mona was his mother, and he probably wanted to talk to her about something personal.

"What's wrong?" Bailey asked as she pulled away from the house.

She turned startled eyes on her boss. "What do you mean?"

"You seem flustered. Did something happen?"

"No." Sierra pressed her lips together and faced forward. Bailey did not need to know how nutty her assistant behaved. She hoped to be given more responsibility soon and being an unprofessional busybody was not the way to get it.

"Okay." Bailey went on to talk about the project they were headed to.

Sierra forced her focus on the job ahead, but a nagging thought nipped at the back of her mind. Something was up with John. But what?

Spencer could not get Trey off his mind. The teen truly appeared to despise him. Spencer could handle not being liked by everyone, but the idea of the teen hating him because of what had happened didn't set well. He had to find a way for them to make peace. He knew firsthand what kind of damage festering hate could do. He'd seen it in some of the people he'd arrested.

Not knowing Trey put him at a disadvantage, but he wasn't a quitter. He'd find a way to make friends with and get through to the teen. He gazed out the window of his house in Sunriver, unable to see beyond the glass into the night. He shook his head and closed the worn out drapes.

One day, he'd like to update this home. He'd

purchased it five years ago with that in mind. It'd been a turnkey property and he'd yet to put his own touch on the place. That was it! He'd renovate with the help of a designer and said designer would be Sierra. But that only solved half of his problem. How would he reach out to Trey and clear the air between them? Maybe Mark would have an idea.

He grabbed his cell phone and speed dialed his buddy and fellow police officer. "Hey, it's Spencer. Do you have a minute?"

"Sure. What's up?"

"Remember that teen I told you about earlier?"

"From the silent alarm house? Sure. What about him?"

"I know I shouldn't let it bother me, and I probably ought to let this go, but it's eating at me. I want to make it up to him. I'd feel bad if he hates cops for the rest of his life because of me."

"That's a heavy burden. Let me talk to Nicole. Maybe she'll have an idea. Her teacher's mind comes up with all sorts of things that I never would have considered for almost anything."

Spencer chuckled. "That sounds about right. I should've gone straight to your wife."

"I like that you came to me first. Hold on a sec. I'll get her."

"Hello, Spencer," Nicole said.

"Hi."

"Mark tells me you made a mess of something and need my help."

He winced. "Afraid so." He explained the situation then waited. The line was too quiet. "Are you still there?"

"Yes, just thinking. Teenage boys aren't exactly my

sweet spot. I work with younger kids."

"I know, but I don't know who else to turn to. This is really important to me."

"I understand. I'll do my best, but you've been warned. What about putting together a community event through the police department? Positive press is always a good thing for the police."

"I like where you're going with this. Any idea what we should do?"

"A run, a pizza feed, a dance?"

He rubbed his stubbly chin. "Those all sound like a lot of work. I'm not sure I'd get much support considering the load everyone is already carrying."

She chuckled. "Sorry. I should've thought of that."

"No need to apologize. I'll think on it. Maybe something less involved will come to me." No idea was bad as far as he was concerned.

"I had another thought," she continued. "What about a mentoring program through the police department? I know Mark would want to get involved."

"Like a big brother, big sister kind of thing?"

"Uh-huh."

"I like that."

"You do realize it will be even more work to pull off than my other ideas since it's long term?"

"Yes. However, I see huge value in this idea." But what if he went to all the work to set up the program, and Trey didn't want anything to do with it?

CHAPTER FIVE

MONDAY MORNING SIERRA RUSHED OUT THE front door. She needed to stop by Brewed Awakenings to get Bailey's usual mocha on her way to work. She dropped her keys and nearly growled in frustration. She should have left fifteen minutes ago. This was not like her. She was Miss Organized, yet somehow she'd forgotten to turn on her alarm and had overslept.

A police cruiser pulled up behind her car with Spencer at the wheel. "Again?" She plastered on a smile. There was no sense in making an enemy of the local police. Besides, she couldn't fault Spencer for trying to make amends. She only wished he'd let it go.

Spencer got out and raised a hand in greeting. "Good morning."

"Well, it's morning anyway," she mumbled. "What brings you by? Again," she added softly.

He frowned. "Sorry. Is this a bad time?"

"It is. I'm running late. Is there something I can help you with?" She juggled her purse, phone, magazines and a travel mug before dropping her cell phone.

"Rough morning?" Spencer bent and picked up her phone.

"Thanks. And yes. I overslept." She tucked the phone into her jacket pocket.

He glanced toward the house. "Is your son around?"

"Trey is in the shower, then he has online school." She moved to her car and pressed the unlock button. She reached for the handle, and the travel mug she had balanced on a stack of magazines wobbled.

"Let me help." He grabbed the mug then pulled open the door for her. "I'm here for a couple of reasons, but they will keep."

"Oh. Okay." Now she *really* wanted to know what was going on. "Care to give me a hint as to what this is about?"

He grinned. "Sure. I'm looking to update my house, and I'm in need of an interior designer."

"I see." Relief surged through her. Business she could handle. Her son's words about the cop being interested in her had sprung to mind, and it was a relief he was not here on a personal mission. She reached for her purse and pulled out a business card for Belafonte Design then handed it to him. "Give me a call later, and I'll set up an appointment for you with Bailey. She's the lead designer."

"What about you?"

"Me?" Unease gripped her. "I don't understand."

"Aren't you a designer too?"

"Technically, yes, but I work for Belafonte Design. As an employee there I can't freelance."

"That's too bad. I'll give you a call later to set up an appointment."

"Sounds great. If you'll excuse me, I really need to get going." She clicked her seatbelt into place while looking pointedly at the car door that Spencer rested his hand on.

"Oh, sorry." He pushed the door closed then marched back to the police cruiser.

She watched in her rearview mirror as he backed out then followed. She was so late it was ridiculous. At least

Bailey was a nice boss and wouldn't hold being late this once against her. She got behind a car going just below the twenty-five mile per hour speed limit. Of all days! At the next circle, when the slow car went one way, she branched in the opposite direction from normal taking a chance it would be faster.

Her cell phone rang. She answered it with her car's blue tooth. "This is Sierra."

"Oh, good. I'm glad I caught you," Bailey said. "Have you gone to the coffee shop yet?"

"No. I'm running very late."

"Not a problem. This works to our advantage. We have a big client coming in this morning, and I was hoping you'd pick up some muffins and whatever else looks good."

"Would you like me to go to Hot Lava Bakery and Coffee then? Or get what they have at Brewed Awakenings?"

"Whatever is easier for you. I can make tea and coffee here today."

"Are you saying you don't want a mocha?"

Bailey chuckled. "It's hard to believe, but yes. I'm addicted to those things, and I need to cut back."

"Sure thing, boss. I'll be there in about thirty minutes." Since she'd begun working for Belafonte Design, they had switched office locations a few times and were now back at Mona's house, the matriarch of the family's home office. It was a beautiful house in the middle of the woods and closer than the family offices in Bend, so this location worked well for her current living situation.

She finally pulled into the parking lot and rushed into the bakery. Relief coursed through her when only one person stood in line ahead of her.

He glanced over his shoulder, then an easy smile crossed his face as he turned to face her. "Hey, we met the other day at Mrs. Drake's place."

"Carl, right?"

"Good memory. Remember to give me a call if you have any trouble."

"I will. Thanks." A moment later she placed her order, including a chai tea latte for herself. She generally didn't buy a special drink, but she needed one today. The past several days had been challenging. Too bad she didn't have time to relax while enjoying the treat. On her way out, she waved to Carl, who sat at a table near the window.

Twenty minutes later, she sat across from Bailey in her office, the chai tea latte long gone.

"Mr. and Mrs. Plato will be coming in shortly," Bailey said. "They recently purchased an older house and want to renovate before moving in. They have a sizable budget. I went by their home on Friday to catch their vision and take measurements." She turned her computer screen around to face Sierra. "What do you think?" Her eyes glowed with excitement.

Sierra studied the kitchen layout and nodded her approval. "Did Belafonte Construction get hired too, or will we be working with another company?"

Bailey nodded. "Belafonte Construction will be doing the job." She clicked a button and a new screen popped up. "What do you think of the master suite?"

"I like it. The ceiling beams are a nice touch."

Bailey clicked through every room in the house then sat back grinning. "I spent my entire weekend working on this."

"You should've called. I could have helped."

Bailey shrugged. "Stephen helped."

Sierra sucked in her bottom lip and bit down to keep from saying something she'd regret, like why wouldn't Bailey trust her with a design? She graduated at the top of her class, and her professors spoke highly of her work. Although grateful to be working in her desired field, she'd hoped to be given more responsibility by now.

"What's wrong?" Bailey's brows furrowed. "Did you see something that concerned you?" She stared at the computer screen.

"No. Nothing like that." She took a deep breath and let it out in a puff. "May I be honest?"

"Of course."

"I'm disappointed that you didn't ask for my help."

"Oh." Bailey frowned. "I honestly never considered bothering you on your days off, other than to drop by the stuff I needed you to order. You'd just moved, and you seemed a little discombobulated last week when I stopped over. I didn't think you'd be up to helping me."

"When you put it like that, I guess your decision makes sense. So tell me more about what you're doing."

Relief covered Bailey's face. "It's a huge project, and the biggest one this company has ever been hired to do according to Stephen. I'll probably need to assign you to any smaller projects that come in until this is at a point where it doesn't need my full attention."

Sierra sat up taller and couldn't help grinning. This was exactly what she'd been waiting for. "What do you have for me?"

Bailey looked back at her with sad green eyes. "Uh.

Well, I don't have anything at the moment. I'm not comfortable handing off something I'm already working on, but you know how this business is. A new contract is right around the corner. Don't worry."

"Sure. Sounds good." Sierra couldn't keep the disappointment from her voice. She'd really hoped Bailey had a job to pass along to her. When she'd taken this position Bailey had warned her it would be like this, but she'd believed deep down that she could prove her worth as a designer and have clients of her own by now.

The office phone rang. Sierra answered on the second ring. "Belafonte Design. Sierra speaking." She glanced toward Bailey, who busily sorted through fabric samples.

"Hi, it's Spencer. Officer Preston." He quickly added. "I was calling to speak with Bailey."

"One minute please." She put the call on hold and held the phone out to Bailey. "Spencer Preston would like to speak with you." Her heart rate kicked up a notch. Could this be the break she'd hoped for?

"That's odd. He never calls. Thanks." She picked up the phone. "Spence, what's up?"

Sierra stood to leave the room and give them privacy.

"You're sure?" Bailey said.

Sierra paused in the doorway, brushing away a non-existent cobweb.

"That's fine." She wrote something on the calendar then disconnected the call.

"Sierra, it looks as if your wish has come true. Spencer has requested you as his designer."

Sierra whirled around to face her boss. Bailey didn't look angry or put out, but rather she looked happy. "I won't let you down."

"I know you won't. But I expect you to run everything by me before you present your proposal to him. You have a meeting at his home this evening. I hope that won't be a problem." She handed her a sticky note with an address and phone number on it. "Don't be late."

Sierra nodded. "The timing is fine." It was finally happening. She had her first client. She bit back a grin and a squeal of delight, not wanting to show too much excitement and run the risk of looking unprofessional. Too bad it was Spencer, because she was still a little miffed over what happened last week. But, as they say, beggars couldn't be choosers. Now she needed to somehow get over her annoyance with the officer for what he did to her son.

Spencer rushed around his house picking up the laundry and clutter. He'd impulsively asked to have Sierra stop by this evening without thinking about how messy his place was, and he'd been working all day. A knock sounded on the door. He tossed the laundry basket filled with mismatched socks and piles of mail into the laundry room and closed the door. At least the kitchen was clean.

He hustled to the door and pulled it open. "Right on time. Come in, Sierra."

She carried a large laptop-type bag. "Thanks." She stood in the tiny entryway and looked around. "Nice place."

"It has good bones, but it's long past time to bring it into the twenty-first century. I think the kitchen dates back to the seventies."

She shuddered. "Not that." She shot him a grin as she stepped further into his two-story home. According to Bailey, the second level was more like a loft, but it held a guest bedroom and bathroom.

"Should we start in the kitchen?"

"Is that the room you want to update?"

"Yes, but I think it would also be nice to put in new flooring and a fresh coat of paint and something new on the windows throughout this level. These drapes are getting threadbare and the light filters through."

"That's a great idea. What's your budget?"

"Fifty thousand."

She nodded. "What's the square footage of your place?"

"This level is twelve hundred and the loft is six."

"Did you want any work done up there?"

"Yes, but I don't think there's enough in the budget for that."

"I'll take measurements and see what we can do. If we are using the same footprint, you'd be surprised how far your money can stretch. It's all in the finishes." They discussed design and exactly what he wanted. She took measurements and photos of the spaces. A worried look covered her face.

"What's the matter?"

"Nothing."

"You're sure? Is the budget too low? I know cabinets are pricy. I'm willing to use stock as long as they're solid wood and you can make them look custom. But there is no salvaging these things. They are in bad shape."

She nodded. "I think we can make the budget work

for the guest bath, kitchen, flooring and drapes. But it will depend how expensive your choices are. Let's talk details. Do you have any idea what kind of countertops you want?"

He would never admit this to her, but he enjoyed watching the home improvement shows and had binged on them over the weekend looking for inspiration for this place. "I like quartz. I know a lot of people prefer granite, but the maintenance is more than I want to deal with."

"You know countertops?" Surprise lit her voice. "I'm impressed."

His neck heated.

She asked him several more questions before closing her laptop. "Barring any surprises, like water damage from leaky pipes, the budget should be adequate." They discussed flooring options and settled on carpet in the bedrooms, but the rest was still to be determined.

"When would you like to meet to go over the proposal?" Sierra asked.

"I don't work Thursday or Friday."

"I'll have something ready by Friday then. I'll be in touch."

"Sounds good." He walked her to the door and let her out. Disappointment coursed through him. Somehow he thought this would have gone differently. He'd imagined there'd be a spark or something between them and not a spark of animosity like the first time they'd met—he was no romantic, but he was lonely and liked Sierra.

She'd seemed pre-occupied this evening. Could something be going on at home? He shook off the thought. His job made him cynical about life in general, and he didn't want to be that way toward Sierra. An air of mystery surrounded her. For example, her age perplexed him. There was no way she was old enough to be Trey's birth mother. What was the story there? Had she adopted him? If not, he definitely favored his dad in looks. He would never have connected Trey and Sierra based on their features.

Ever since Mark and Nicole had gotten married a few months ago, they'd been trying to play matchmaker, although they were lousy at it. He wanted to settle down and marry, but the right woman had never come along. Not that he hadn't dated—he'd had his heart broken. What was he thinking? Why would he want to risk that again? The last woman he'd been serious about, he'd thought was *the one*. He'd even considered proposing until he found out she'd been seeing another guy the entire time they'd been together. Apparently, she was just having fun, which would have been nice to know sooner rather than later.

He'd thought he read people well up to the day he'd found out she wasn't serious about him. He was glad he found out before he'd proposed and made a fool of himself. Although interested in Sierra, he wasn't looking to have his heart broken, so he'd better tread lightly where she was concerned.

His cell phone beeped. He swiped the screen. "Spencer speaking."

"Hi, it's Sierra. I hate to bother you, but I have a little problem."

He stood taller. "What's wrong?"

"I had a blowout. I don't know how to change a tire, and I let my auto club membership expire."

"Where are you?"

He almost laughed at her response. She was only three

to four hundred feet from his place. "I'll be right there. Do you have a lug wrench and jack?"

"I think so. But I'm not positive."

"I'll bring mine, just in case." He'd be sure to teach her how to change a tire while he was at it. There was no sense in driving such a short distance. He shrugged into his jacket, grabbed the tools from behind the seat of his pickup along with a flashlight. It would be pitch black soon.

A shiver ran up his spine. Sunriver's temps were always too cold for him. He preferred summer temps, but spring here had a lot of variety when it came to weather, which he liked for the most part.

He spotted Sierra ahead. It looked like he was getting a second chance with her tonight. Maybe the conversation would play to his favor this time.

CHAPTER SIX

"I'M GOING TO BE LATER THAN I'd planned, Trey. Do you mind starting dinner? We're having spaghetti." Sierra paced back and forth trying to stay warm as she waited for Spencer to come to her rescue. The man had impressed her this evening—he knew what he wanted, and she liked that.

"Fine. What's wrong?" Trey asked.

"Why do you ask that?"

"Your voice. You sound worried."

Her son knew her too well. "I had a blowout. Officer Preston is going to put the spare on for me, then I'll come straight home."

"Did you crash? Are you okay?" Panic filled his voice.

"I'm fine. Don't worry. I was barely out of his street when it happened so I wasn't going fast."

"You were at his house?"

"I'll explain when I get home."

"Are you dating him?"

"No." She almost snapped, but caught herself in time and used her patient mom voice instead. "I need to go. I see him coming. I shouldn't be too long. Please keep dinner warm for me." She disconnected the call. Whew. Her son had sounded very bothered by the thought of her dating Spencer. Was it only Spencer, or would he be bothered if she dated anyone? What did it matter? She wasn't interested in giving her heart to another man only to have him walk out when things got tough. She pocketed her cell phone. "Hey, Spencer. Thanks for rescuing me."

"Just doing my job."

She scrunched her nose. "Now I'm really sorry, since you're off duty."

"Don't worry about it. Helping people is what I do, and I enjoy it." He grinned and raised a brow. "No one ever taught you how to change a tire, huh?"

"'Fraid not."

"Today's your lucky day. I'm going to walk you through it, but before I do you better turn on your emergency flashers. I don't want either of us to get hit while we're changing the tire.

Her brain froze. *Walk her through it?* "You mean *I'm* going to change it?" She flicked on the hazard lights.

He nodded. "If this had happened out in the middle of nowhere, what would you have done? You need to know how to change your own tire."

Of course he was right, but she wasn't dressed for it, and her fingers were near freezing. She held in a groan and pulled an old utility blanket from the backend of her SUV. At least she could lay it on the ground and not get too dirty.

A Jeep pulled up behind her SUV. A broad-shouldered man got out and sauntered toward them. It was too dark to see his face clearly. "Sierra? Is everything okay?"

She knew that voice. "John?" He finally got close enough that she could see his face. She didn't expect to see him out here.

"She's fine. It was only a minor blowout." Spencer

handed her a weird looking tool.

"What do I do with this?" She asked

John laughed. "You use it to remove the lug nuts. That's a lug wrench." He reached for the tool.

Spencer stepped forward. "No, let her do it. She needs to learn."

John narrowed his eyes, clearly annoyed. "We haven't met." He held out his hand. "I'm John Belafonte."

Spencer grasped his hand. "Spencer Preston. I hired your company to do a remodel in my house. This happened as Sierra was leaving after our design meeting."

John visibly relaxed. "It's good to meet you. I remember talking on the phone. I'm the contractor for the job at your house."

Sierra's pulse accelerated. Even though she knew it was a possibility they'd work together, this confirmed it.

"You're a cop, right?" John asked.

"I am." Spencer spread his legs and rested his hands at his waist as if ready for battle.

"That's cool. Thanks for what you do," John said.

Spencer relaxed his stance and glanced toward Sierra. "We should get started before it's too dark to see what you're doing."

"Oh, okay." She'd been so fascinated by watching the interplay between the men, she almost forgot about changing the tire. Spencer put the jack into place for her as she squatted beside him and the back-passenger tire and watched. It didn't look too complicated, but she prayed she'd never have to find out for herself. She definitely needed to reinstate her auto club membership.

"Slide the wrench over a lug nut."

She did as Spencer directed.

"Good. Now twist it," he said.

She tried but couldn't make it budge.

"Put a little weight into it," John suggested.

She grunted as she pulled with everything she had — nothing.

John nudged past Spencer and placed his hand beside hers. "Try again."

She nearly fell over as it easily moved this time.

"How'd you do that?" She looked at his large biceps and swallowed. Okay, stupid question.

Spencer cleared his throat. She caught his eye and noticed he looked slightly put out. It was probably not a good idea to get on the local law enforcement's bad side, or for that matter, her new client's bad side. "I've got this, John. Thanks for the help."

He took a step back. "Sure thing. See you." He waved.

She raised a hand. He was a nice guy and certainly knew his way around a lug wrench.

"You ready to try the next one?" Spencer asked.

The rest of the nuts came off easily and before she knew it, the full size spare was in place and ready to be tightened. She did the honors, but Spencer tightened them up a little more. Panic gripped her. "I hope you didn't make it so tight I can't get them off."

"You shouldn't have a problem," Spencer said. He shined a light onto her tire. "Hmm."

"What?"

"Nothing. I'm surprised that this blew since it appears to be in good condition."

"Don't freak accidents happen all the time?"

"I wouldn't go that far, but yes, they happen. I'm glad you were here when it blew out."

"Me too. Thanks for rescuing me."

"My pleasure." Spencer stood and brushed off his jeans.

Interesting. He'd gone from 'doing his job' to his pleasure. She couldn't help feeling good about that—although she had no idea why. "I should head home. Trey is keeping my dinner warm."

"Sure. Hey, speaking of dinner. You want to grab a bite sometime?"

She stopped. "Like a date?"

He nodded.

"I don't date. Remember?" She tossed the blanket into the back and rushed to the driver's side door.

"Seriously? I thought your son was just saying that. Why don't you date?" He followed her.

"It's a personal choice. See you Friday." Her heart pounded as she climbed inside. Every instinct telling her to punch the gas, she instead eased away from the side of the road. What was she so afraid of? Spencer was one of the good guys—at least he seemed to be from what she knew of him. She'd have said the same of Randy though.

Had Spencer only hired her as a way to get close so he could ask her out? That would be extreme and mighty expensive all things considered. So what if he had? It wasn't like she could do anything about it. Besides, he'd done her a favor, and she certainly wasn't going to back out now. But what if he no longer wanted her on the job? She'd never get her own projects if her first client fired her.

Friday morning, Spencer stood in his kitchen with Sierra, looking over the design plan she'd come up with. "I can afford this?" It didn't seem possible. Everything looked so high end.

She nodded. "The stock cabinetry helped. If we had gone with custom cabinets, there's no way we could do everything you want. We also have a contingency fund in case something comes up."

"Hopefully it's enough." As much as he wanted and needed to do this update to his kitchen, he'd seen enough remodeling shows to know that things rarely went as planned.

"Bailey and Stephen were confident we'd be okay."

He nodded and noticed she seemed nervous. Maybe it was time to clear the air. "About the other night when I asked you to dinner. I don't want that to make things awkward. I'm a big boy and can take rejection."

Her gaze shot to his and held. "I wasn't rejecting *you*. I seriously don't date. It really has nothing to do with you personally."

It felt personal, but her words helped dull the sting of her rejection. "I'm still curious why you don't date."

"I can see you're not going to drop this until I answer your question. I'm a single mom, and I've made some mistakes I don't care to repeat. My son is the most important person in my life. He's a good kid, and I don't want to mess that up by bringing a man into the picture." A pained look crossed her face. "Although it looks like I might not have much choice."

He leaned against the Formica countertop. "What do you mean?"

She shook her head. "I shouldn't have said anything.

You're a client. You don't need to hear about my problems."

"Please don't let the fact that you are my decorator stop you. I'm curious, and I'd like to help if there's any way I can. You said you might not have a choice. Is someone harassing you? I'm a cop, and I hope we can be friends, so if there's anything I can do . . ." He tried to remain nonchalant, but something in the tone of her voice said this was big. "You want coffee?" He motioned toward a wire carousel of pods. "I'm working my way through all the different flavor options." Afraid she wouldn't take him up on his offer to keep talking, he pulled a mug from the counter, grabbed one that said mocha, and popped it into the machine.

"Do you have chai tea?"

He twirled to the backside. "I'm not a fan of tea, so you're doing me a favor." He waited for his to brew, then popped in the chai tea pod. When hers was finished he handed her the mug. "Let's take a seat. It's warm enough today to sit outside." He pulled the slider open and brushed off two of the white plastic chairs. "They're not pretty, but they do the job."

She sat. "Thanks. Too bad there's not money in the budget for new patio furniture. I saw a great set on sale the other day, and I've always wanted to design an outdoor space," she said in a wistful tone.

"I hope you get to someday. Back to why you don't have a choice about a man being in your life." He didn't like the sound of anyone having someone forced upon them, especially Sierra. He liked her, what little he knew of her that is.

She took a sip of the tea. "This is really good."

He could wait her out, as long as she didn't flee first. Something told him this could be important. He swallowed some of his mocha then set it on the plastic table that matched the chairs.

"I suppose there's no harm in telling you since you asked. You might even be able to help me."

He rested an ankle on his knee. "I will if I can."

"I'm a very private person, and I would appreciate if this stays between us."

"I'm a police officer first and foremost, so—"

"Because you're a cop, I'm going to tell you. I had Trey when I was sixteen. My boyfriend, Randy, was a year older than me, but not mature enough to be a dad. We tried to make a go of raising Trey together, but he wasn't interested in being a parent and resented Trey and me. His parents were not supportive of us, and shortly after Trey's first birthday they sold their house and moved away— Randy went with them. Things were not healthy between us. In retrospect, it was for the best that he left, but at the time it felt like anything but. I've not seen or heard from him or any of his family since." She sighed. "Now Trey wants to meet him. I don't know where to start to find him, or even if I should. What if Randy refuses to meet Trey or worse yet, agrees to meet him then walks away again?"

His insides wrenched. She was in a tough spot. It stank that her son was bound to get hurt no matter what happened. All the more reason he needed to work on that big brother/big sister idea. "When you say things were not good between you, will you be specific?" Something in the tone of her voice sent his cop instincts on alert.

Her face heated. "He had a temper," she mumbled.

"He hurt you?"

She shrugged. "Only once, but it was an accident."

Fat chance. "Why would you even consider looking for him?"

"He's Trey's dad. My son is practically grown now, and Randy's temper was related to the predicament he found himself in. Being a teen parent is not fun or easy. He wasn't mature enough to handle it. I know it sounds like denial when I say him hurting me was an accident, but it really was. Granted it would never have happened had he not been so frustrated with Trey's constant crying."

"Tell me what happened." Anger simmered right below the surface. The man had done Sierra and her son a favor by leaving. Her logic made no sense to him, and he had zero tolerance for abusers.

"It was nothing really. I shouldn't have even brought it up. He'd had as much crying as he could take and attempted to storm out of the house. I jumped in his way to try and stop him, but he was a rock. He couldn't stop fast enough and knocked me to the ground. When I fell I hit my head. But it was an accident."

"Okay. I see your point." Although he wasn't convinced the man wasn't a threat. "It's been a long time since you last saw him. You have no way of knowing what kind of man he turned out to be."

"True, but what am I supposed to do?"

"I know someone who specializes in finding people. He owes me one. I'll check Randy out first and see if he's someone you can trust."

"You'd do that for me? Why?"

"It's my job."

She shook her head. "No, it's not."

"Fine. I want to help. I don't want to see you hurt, either."

"Thank you, but I don't want to be indebted to you. I thought maybe you could look through police records or something. Forget I ever mentioned Randy."

He raised a brow. "He's in the system?" She hadn't mentioned her boyfriend had a criminal record. But he shouldn't be surprised after what she'd told him.

"No. At least not that I know of. Does that mean you can't find him without your friend's help?"

"I'm going to help you one way or another, but first you need to decide if you really want to find this man. Seriously consider all the possibilities. Are you willing to share your son with him? Are you ready to face whatever comes from introducing Trey to his dad? What if he wants to share custody? What if he still has a temper?"

"Randy gave up his parental rights before leaving. I still have the signed paperwork. There is no way he will ever be alone with Trey. I won't allow it."

She was naïve if she thought she could keep the boy away from his dad when she wasn't around. It wasn't like Trey was a kid. "I'd like to see the paperwork. It should have the information I need. You're sure about this?"

"No, not really. I'm glad to know you can help me, but let's not do anything yet. I want to pray about it first."

"You're a Christian?"

"I am. Are you?"

"No. But Mark is." He had been hounding him to visit his church for months. He had to admit to being curious. Mark had a peace about him that Spencer envied. "Do you go to church?"

"Trey and I attend one in Bend. I noticed Bailey and

Stephen go there too, although I rarely see them since we usually go to the early service and Bailey doesn't like to rise early."

He nodded. "I know the place." Sierra must be a morning person. She did seem perkier this morning than Monday evening. "I think I received a flier in the mail about a guest speaker doing a Bible prophecy seminar."

"Yes. I saw that too."

"Are you going to go?" The topic interested him more than he cared to admit. He'd even thought to attend, and it would be nice to see a familiar face there.

"I might."

"We could go together if you decide to."

Unease covered her face.

"Not as a date," he quickly added. "Just two people carpooling to the same place."

"Hmm. We could do that." Her face turned pensive. "But you aren't Trey's favorite person. Maybe driving together would be a bad idea."

CHAPTER SEVEN

SIERRA PULLED UP BESIDE JOHN'S JEEP in the driveway of his mother's house. He rarely came to the house, yet he'd come more than once recently in a short amount of time — odd. Although, considering his mom seldom left the house, she shouldn't be too surprised to see him. Mona only ventured downstairs if one of her sons carried her, but Stephen felt it was good for her to have people in the house.

Personally, Sierra was glad the older woman rarely made her presence known. The few times she'd had contact with Mona, she had been snippy, and Sierra didn't care to be snapped at. Bailey was sweet, though, and a pleasure to work for. She hustled inside.

John stood near the entryway. He raised a brow. "Good morning."

"Hi. What brings you by?"

"You."

Her heart hammered in her chest. "Me?" Her voice raised a notch. Had she done something wrong, or was this personal?

"Rick has his hands full and asked me to go over the design for the cop's house with you."

"Oh. So you really *are* a contractor?" Sure, Bailey had said he would be working with her as the contractor on Spencer's place, and he'd said as much himself when he stopped to help with her tire, but she still had a hard time wrapping her brain around him doing manual labor. He always ran the office.

"I know my way around a construction site. You couldn't grow up in this house and not." He grinned. "Do you have the plans with you?"

"I stayed up late and worked on them. They're on my computer. Give me a minute to get organized, then I'll run through everything with you."

He followed her to the office on the first level of the massive house. This place was grander than the one she was currently living in. Even the wood floors looked nicer. "Where's Bailey?"

"With Rick and Stephen working on the Plato place. I doubt you'll be seeing much of her for the next several weeks. She's doing a couple of feature walls with stencils and insisted on doing the work herself. I guess she didn't trust anyone else." He rubbed the back of his neck. "Rick is miffed with me for taking on Spencer's place when he was already slammed with the other project."

"Really? But I thought the plan was to . . ." It didn't matter what she thought. "Never mind. Should we hire someone else to help?" She ducked her head. That was probably not the smartest thing to say.

"You don't think I can do the job?" He crossed his arms.

"I didn't say that. I'm only concerned about your relationship with your brother. If working outside the business office is going to cause problems—"

"Let me worry about Rick." He relaxed enough to stuff his hands into his jeans pockets. "We've always been a little too competitive. He doesn't like me stepping in where he's top dog. That's all." He chuckled. "I may be rusty, but I'll get the job done, and I'll make sure it's done right. Your cop friend is in good hands."

"He's not my friend." Now why had she said that? Spencer sure acted like a friend, and there was nothing wrong with counting him as a friend, so long as she didn't grow dependent on him. That would be a huge mistake. She'd learned a long time ago to only depend on herself and the Lord because people didn't stick around.

"Oh. My mistake. Guess I assumed since he was helping with your tire."

"He was the only person I knew to call, and he was close." She opened the file with Spencer's design and clicked print. There was no need to have John looking over her shoulder as she walked him through what they were going to do. He made her nervous. He was truly the most attractive of the three brothers with his dark wavy hair, light blue eyes, and broad shoulders.

The printer spat out several sheets of paper. She walked over and gathered them then handed the proposal to John. "How about you take a look and then we can discuss any concerns or questions you have?"

"Sure." He eased onto the small sofa and flipped through the pages. "This looks straight forward. Rick already has a crew assembled and they're ready to start on Monday. Will that work?"

"Let me check." She sent a text to Spencer and waited for his reply. "Are you sure you are up for this, John? This is my first real job, and I don't want anything to go wrong."

"Thanks for your faith in me," he said drily. "For the record, something usually goes wrong on most projects, but I'm good at working through issues, so relax and trust me to do my job. I might not have worked side-by-side with my brothers for a long time, but I've done this before."

She nodded as her phone dinged. She checked the text. "Spencer says that's fine and to stop by his place the evening before for the key. He starts work early and won't be home when we get there."

A sheepish look covered his face. "Can you do that for me? I have plans that night."

She resisted rolling her eyes. "Of course, but how will I get it to you?" She shook her head. "Never mind. I'll be at his place in the morning too. I want to walk you through the plans onsite before you start work."

"Or," he drew the word out. "We could meet for coffee first then head over to the house?" He tipped his head to one side and raised a brow. "I always start my day with a cup of joe."

She pressed her lips together. His boyish charm drew her in. No good could come of meeting at the coffee shop. Then again, they did need to establish a rapport if they were going to work together. "I guess. Or we could plan to meet a little earlier at Spencer's house."

"Coffee will be more fun. Don't you think?"

Was John flirting with her? She wasn't sure how she felt about that—flattered, excited, scared? All three? He was certainly good looking and successful, grounded, a Christian, and from what she'd heard he was a good person. It was one thing to be attracted to him but another to act on that attraction. For so many years she'd shied away from men and the complications they brought with them. Did she even have the ability to put herself out there again and risk her heart? She'd told herself through the years that all men were not like Randy, but it was still hard.

"Sierra?" John looked at her with concern in his baby blue eyes. "We can meet at the house if getting coffee first is a problem."

"No. It's fine. I like to treat myself to a chai tea now and then." Although she'd been doing that a lot recently.

He grinned. "Great. But if something changes, call me." He pulled a business card from his wallet and wrote his cell number on the back.

"I will. See you then." Her heart thundered in her chest. It was no big deal, but it felt huge.

For the first time in years, rather than wearing slacks and a nice shirt to work, John tugged on jeans and flannel. He'd picked up a couple pairs of work gloves and dug out his old tool belt from when he'd labored alongside his dad years ago. Anticipation filled him so much that coffee was probably not a good idea, but he wouldn't pass up the opportunity to visit with Sierra even if a dose of caffeine was ill advised.

He whistled as he palmed his keys then headed for the door of his studio apartment. Most people found it hard to believe that after growing up in a virtual mansion he'd chosen to live in a tiny studio apartment, but it was easier. He had little to tie him down, and since his place was so small, no one ever wanted to come over, which suited him fine—at least it used to. Even though he'd turned into a neat freak recently and wouldn't mind uninvited guests, no one ever dropped in.

He'd been living here since his early twenties, but now at thirty-three it felt stifling. Change was definitely in the air. From his place in Bend, it'd take him about twenty-five minutes to get to the coffee shop in the Sunriver Village. He'd be right on time.

The drive on 97 from Bend to Sunriver was pleasantly uneventful, and he pulled into the parking lot. He got out and strode toward Sierra's SUV, a couple of spots away.

She waved and quickly slid from her vehicle, wearing dark-wash jeans and a flowing pink blouse and navy blazer. "Good morning. I was reviewing the plans one more time." She eased up beside him, and they walked toward Brewed Awakenings.

"I'm sure you have nothing to worry about," he said hoping to ease her mind. She was clearly nervous. That made two of them. It'd been a long time since he'd done construction, and he'd never been on his own with a crew. However, he spent enough time on job sites to know how things were done.

She pulled a key with a red ribbon attached to it from her jeans pocket. "I added the ribbon. I thought it'd be too easy to lose otherwise."

"Good idea." He pulled the door open. "After you."

She breezed past him, and he caught a whiff of her vanilla-scented perfume. "I'm thinking we should get our drinks and go," she suggested. "That will give us time to run through everything on site before the crew shows up."

Disappointment hit him—talk about a letdown from the high he'd been on. He'd hoped to get to know her, not talk shop, but he had to respect her boundaries. "Sure.

That's probably for the best since we haven't worked together before."

Relief showed on her face. She turned and placed her order. He'd planned to treat her, but the line had been clearly drawn. He ordered a small caramel macchiato, and they stood along the wall waiting for their drinks. "Are you excited about your first solo design job?"

She looked up at him with a grin, though her eyes remained pensive. "Yes, but I'm mostly nervous. I have ice cubes for fingers." She touched them to his arm. "See." She stuffed her hands into her jeans pockets. "I've always been like this when I get nervous. It's annoying."

He shifted to the other foot and felt himself relax. "I've seen your design, and I don't think you have anything to be nervous about. Spencer requested you, so he obviously likes your work."

She shook her head. "I don't know how. He's never seen it. I think he asked for me simply because we got off to a rough start when we first met, and he's trying to make it up to me."

His eyes widened. "Wow! What did he do that he's willing to spend fifty thousand dollars to make up for it?"

The barista called her name then his a later.

"Okay, when you put it like that, I feel silly for thinking he requested me to make up for what happened. I'll tell you about it sometime, but not here." She motioned to the crowd around him. "I respect law enforcement, and I don't want to say something that would reflect badly on him."

"Good enough." They walked to the parking lot together then parted company. He liked that she was unwilling to speak negatively about Spencer in public. It showed the kind of trait that a lot of people lacked—integrity.

A short time later he pulled up to the project house and parked beside Sierra's SUV. She stood at the hood sipping her drink. He got out with his coffee and strode toward her. "Let's get this party started." He pulled out the key and let them inside. "Okay. I see why he wants to remodel."

"It's dated, but by the time we're done, this house will finally enter the twenty-first century." She walked him through exactly what she had planned.

He breathed a sigh of relief. Everything was exactly like he expected, based on the plans, and best of all, she didn't want any walls knocked down. As renovations go, this job would be simple. "Far as I can see, you have nothing to be worried about. The crew will be here in about twenty minutes, and we'll get this place demoed. Where is Spencer staying while this is going on?"

A panicked look covered her pale face. "I think he's staying here. I didn't tell him he should move out." Her words came out in a rush. "I knew I would forget something."

He grasped her shoulders and ducked to her eye level. "It's okay. He can live here while we work. It would have been easier if he wasn't, but we can be flexible."

Her face relaxed. "You're sure?"

"Positive. Although he might decide to stay someplace else on his own. It won't be fun not to have a kitchen."

She nodded.

A knock sounded on the door then it swung open. His team stepped inside.

"That's my cue to leave. Let me know if you have any problems. In the meantime, I'll make sure Spencer is aware of what his living conditions will be like." She greeted the crew on her way out.

As he turned his focus to the job at hand, apprehension sliced through him. It'd been a long time since he'd done construction. Would the crew pick up on his unease? He sure hoped not. At least he'd convinced Sierra he was up to the job. Disappointment still nipped at him that she wasn't interested in spending time outside of work with him. He shook off the thought. He didn't have time to dwell on that right now.

CHAPTER EIGHT

"I CAN'T BELIEVE YOU ARE MAKING me ride in the same car as that cop!" Trey's hands fisted by his sides.

Sierra sucked in a sharp breath. "I didn't realize you'd feel so strongly about this. I'm sorry, but I already told Spencer we could ride together." After thinking it over she figured she was being too cautious and called Spencer to tell him they could carpool. She'd really made a mess of things.

"Mom, please don't make me go with you." The pleading look on his face tore at her. Trey never begged.

"Although I want you to come with us, I will allow you to stay home under one condition." Her palms began to sweat. She'd counted on having her son as a buffer with Spencer. If it was only the two of them, it might feel like a date. No, they were going to church. There was no way that could ever be misinterpreted as a date.

"What's the condition?"

"You need to pray and ask the Lord to help you forgive him so you can move past what happened. Hating him hurts you a lot more than it hurts him. I don't want you to live with hate festering inside you."

"Do you really think he cares about what I think? He's a bully."

"No. He's not. He was doing his job. He did not do anything wrong. You were not harmed and neither was I.

If you want to be angry with someone then blame me. I'm the one who forgot to turn off the alarm."

His shoulders relaxed slightly. "I still don't like him."

"Then stay home and work out your issue. This ends today."

The doorbell chimed. "That will be Spencer." Her heels clicked on the hardwood floor as she crossed from the kitchen into the great room and then the entryway. She pulled the door open and did a double take as a blast of cold air passed over her. She'd never seen him out of uniform—well, except the time she'd gone to the design meeting at his house. He'd been wearing jeans and a T-shirt then, but he looked different now—more appealing.

She took in his neatly combed hair, electric blue button-up shirt and black pants. Okay very appealing. *Ugh!* What was wrong with her lately?

"Hi. Come in for a minute. I need to grab my purse and a jacket."

"No problem. We have plenty of time."

She rushed to the kitchen where her purse sat on the counter and her coat was draped on a chair. "We won't be late. Last chance to come, Trey."

"I'll pass. Is it okay if I watch TV when I'm finished with my homework?"

"Yes." She gave him a quick hug then hustled to where Spencer waited in the entryway. "All set."

He grinned. "Where's Trey?"

"Not coming."

His face fell. "Oh."

She hadn't realized until that moment how important restoring her son's faith in the police or perhaps in himself was to Spencer. She'd need to have a long talk with Trey later. She placed a hand on Spencer's forearm. "Give him time."

"It's fine. I'd hoped he'd gotten over it, is all. I'd hate for him to have negative feelings toward law enforcement because of me." He shrugged. "I guess we should get going."

"Right." She followed him out. He'd parked his long bed pickup as close to the door as possible. Good thing she wore pants. She wouldn't want to have to get into that thing in a dress.

He pulled the door open and offered her a hand up.

She took it and stepped onto the running board then eased inside. The interior was clean—not so much as a gum wrapper littered the cab of his pickup, which seemed odd considering his house had been a little cluttered the first time she'd seen it.

He got in beside her and started the engine. "I feel bad that Trey is missing church because of me." He backed out of her driveway and set out in the direction of the north entrance to Sunriver.

"Don't feel bad. My son is stubborn, and this is on him. He'll come around eventually. Stop worrying. I know Trey, and although he's still holding a grudge, he *will* get over it." At least he better. She would not tolerate his attitude much longer. She prayed he would work it out tonight like she'd told him to.

"Who does he get his stubbornness from?" He glanced her way.

"His mother," she said drily. "Although I don't consider that a flaw. My stubbornness, or determination as I like to call it, is an asset."

He chuckled. "If you say so."

Even though he chuckled she had the feeling he disagreed. "I do. I hope you don't have an issue with my determination."

"No I don't. What gave you that idea?"

Sorry, it's been a rough day and I'm not thinking clearly I guess." Perhaps she was allowing her son's attitude to rub off on her too—not good. She couldn't wait to get to church and really hoped they had a time of worship. Singing always made her feel better, especially when she focused on the Lord rather than herself.

"It's okay. I'm sorry I made you feel judged. I think determination is a quality to be desired. Stubbornness can be an asset in the right circumstances."

"Thank you. I'm glad you see things my way." She shot him a cheeky grin.

They merged onto US 97 heading north toward Bend. She closed her eyes and rested her head against the headrest and prayed that Spencer's life would be touched by tonight's message.

Spencer cast a glance toward Sierra and noted she sat with her eyes closed. She must have had an exhausting day. If she had anything to do with the disaster he'd found at his house, he understood, but even still, she looked fresh in black slacks and a purple top with sleeves that went to just below her elbows. Her blonde hair fell softly around her slightly flushed cheeks. He slid his gaze back to the road.

"You were right about my house."

"What do you mean?" she asked.

"It's going to be difficult to live there while the remodel is going on. I'm glad it's spring and I can grill outside, but . . ."

"But what?" She shifted to face him.

"The water is turned off. So it kind of makes living there a bigger challenge than I realized."

"The water's off?" She sounded surprised. "We aren't moving any pipes. I wonder what's up." She pulled out her cell. "Hey, John, it's Sierra. I'm with Spencer and you're on speaker. He tells me his water is off. Was there a problem?"

"Yeah. I left him a message," John said. "I guess he didn't get it, which explains why he didn't call me back. We had a mishap with the main water line that leads to the house."

"What happened?" Spencer asked.

"I wish I knew. But at some point today the connection at the house was compromised. I asked the crew about it. One person remembers seeing someone in that general area but didn't recognize the guy. I've talked to everyone and no one will admit to damaging the pipe. I'm really sorry, Spencer. This has never happened before."

"Do you think it was deliberately sabotaged?" Spencer's hand tightened on the steering wheel. It didn't sound like an accident to him since there was no reason for anyone to be messing with the water main. His stomach tightened. Could someone he'd put away in the past be messing with him, or did this have to do with the Belafontes?

"To what end? Why would someone do that on purpose? It makes no sense."

"I'm not sure, but something about this bothers me."

"Me too," Sierra added. "Bailey mentioned strange things happening at other sites. Nothing so nefarious though."

"I don't know what's going on," John said. "But it will get fixed. Unfortunately, the plumber Rick said to use is busy until Friday."

"You can't be serious!" Sierra looked ready to pummel someone.

"Afraid so."

"I hope you find whoever is responsible and fire him. And why not use someone else to fix it? There has to be a plumber available sooner. It's ridiculous to wait so long. I'll make some calls and have one there tomorrow."

"No. We need to do this Rick's way."

Spencer admired her fire, but if the look on her face was any indication he needed to jump in before this escalated further. "I was afraid of something like this. I realize the cut line was man-caused, but the plumbing in that house has been a problem from day one. Maybe you can have the wonder plumber check it out."

"I'll have the lines and connections inspected to make sure everything is working as it should, Spencer," John said. "If there are any other problems that need fixed I'll let you know. Don't worry. This is only a hiccup. And Rick says this guy is the best and worth waiting for. So we'll wait as long as you're okay with that."

"It's a pipe. Not rocket science," Sierra mumbled. "I'm sure any plumber will do fine. Do we have money in the budget for this?"

"The pipe will be taken care of at no cost to Spencer. As far as the issues he's having, I'm not sure yet. I'll let you both know as soon as I can."

At least he had a little positive news. "Thanks, man."

"I wish I had something more positive to report."

Sierra sighed. "It's okay. Things happen."

"True. And unless you enjoy roughing it, Spencer, you'll want to find someplace else to stay for the next several days."

"Thanks, John," Sierra said. "Spencer and I are on our way to church to hear that prophecy speaker."

"Oh, yeah. I heard he's supposed to be good."

"That's the best news I've had all day. Well, talk soon. 'Bye." She disconnected the call and tucked her cell into the pocket of her purse. "I'm really sorry about this, Spencer. I've never heard of something like that happening before. But I'm new. Your house is my first real project. I usually only place orders and stuff."

"I'm your first?" He glanced her direction. As much as he wanted to get to know her and her son, maybe hiring an unseasoned designer and contractor was a mistake. Fifty thousand was a ton of money, and he couldn't afford mistakes. Then again the Belafontes had a stellar reputation, so he knew they'd make it right.

"Yes. But don't worry. Everything was approved by both Bailey and Stephen. I allowed for a larger than normal contingency in case problems arise. Not that this will cost you, but, budget wise, you're fine."

"Unless there are more issues."

"I'm sure John would have told me. If any of the plumbing needs worked on, there will more than likely be enough in my contingency fund to cover it. Everything is going to work out. And if you need a place to crash tonight, there's plenty of room at my house. I'm sure Mrs.

Drake wouldn't mind you staying over for one night while you work out accommodations."

"She'd mind and so would Trey."

"Never mind about Trey. He goes to sleep early for a teen. You know Mrs. Drake?"

"Unfortunately, yes." The woman thought she was the queen, and the rest of the world were her subjects. He never enjoyed running into her.

She chuckled. "Ah. Come on. She's not that bad, and she was nice enough to let me and my son housesit for an entire year while she travels."

"Oh, she is that bad. I realize it was a few months ago, but I'm surprised she hired Belafonte Designs. I heard she was in the process of opening her own interior design business." He shook his head. "I must have heard wrong, though. She wouldn't leave the country for a year at the start of a new venture."

"That's news to me. I'm sure you're mistaken. If she's as bad as you say, I seriously doubt she'd allow someone who worked for the competition to live in her house."

"You never know, but I will say no more. I'll take you up on the offer to stay over in the guestroom, but only for tonight. It can be our secret. Speaking of secrets. I found Randy."

Sierra gasped.

CHAPTER NINE

SIERRA STARED INTO THE DARKNESS BEYOND the windows of her house. She hadn't heard a word of the message at church tonight. What was she going to do? She hadn't expected Spencer to find Randy so quickly. The man moved fast. Too fast for her liking.

"You're awake."

Spencer? She whirled around to face him. "Too much on my mind to sleep. What are you doing up. It's past midnight."

"Same. That prophecy speaker gave me a lot to chew on."

She nodded. "What's troubling you?" She walked into the kitchen and put a kettle of water on the stove. Maybe chamomile tea would help her relax.

He sat at the granite-topped island. "It's difficult to believe that events happening in the world today were predicted in the Bible so long ago."

"Makes it hard to doubt there's a God, in my opinion." She pulled two white ceramic mugs from the cupboard. "Do you like herbal tea?"

He shook his head. "But if you think it will help me sleep, then I'm game."

She added a tea bag to each mug. She had so many questions about Randy, but Spencer appeared to have a few questions of his own he needed answered. The kettle whistled, and she poured the boiling water. "There's milk and sugar if you'd like."

"This will be fine. Thanks." He drew the cup to his lips.

"Be careful. It's super hot." She liked to give her tea time to steep and cool.

"Thanks for the heads up." He blew on the liquid. "We know why *I* can't sleep, and I have a strong suspicion I know why you can't. Finding your son's dad is a pretty big deal. You don't have to do anything with the information I gave you."

Her gaze shot to his. Of course, he knew where her head was. He was a cop, and it was part of his job to read people—a survival skill. "I'm considering my options. What can you tell me about him?" She asked. She knew nothing of the man other than what he'd been like more than a decade ago.

"He's married, lives in California, has two kids and a dog."

She crossed her arms. "You forgot the white picket fence." He was living the American dream and left her to fend for their son. Whatever. She didn't want Randy's money, or him, for that matter.

"You sound bitter." Spencer sipped the tea and winced. "You weren't kidding. That burned my tongue even after blowing on it." He set the cup down.

"Sorry. I suppose I do sound like that, but I'm not. Not really. I'm sad for how everything went down, and I'm sad my son doesn't know his dad, but his half-siblings get to have a dad. Does he have a record?"

"No. Only a couple of speeding tickets."

"He always did like to drive fast." He lived life that

way too. Would reconnecting her son with his dad do more harm than good? Definitely not a decision she should be making at this time of night. "I'm going to bed."

"You didn't drink your tea."

"I'll take it with me. Good night, Spencer. Oh, Trey doesn't know you're here, so I'll knock on your door when it's safe to come out in the morning."

"I'll be out of here long before he's up. I start work early."

"Try and get some sleep." She patted him on the shoulder as she passed by. "And thanks for finding Randy."

John spotted Sierra the moment she walked in the front door, and she was not smiling. He'd hoped she would have accepted the plumbing issue and moved on. Apparently not. "Good morning." At least one thing positive came of the situation — Sierra was officially off his suspect list. As angry as she was, there was no way she had anything to do with this. She could be acting, but his gut said her anger was real.

"If you say so. Any news?"

"Nothing has changed from last night." He studied her face. Something more than this project had to be bothering her. She looked deeply distressed. "Everything is under control here, and I could use a coffee break. We can talk about what has you wound up tighter than the strings on that piano." He pointed to a small studio piano in the corner.

Surprise filled her eyes. "I'm not good company today, John, but thanks."

This must be serious. She didn't even deflect his attempt to spend time with her. "That's fine. I'll risk it. Come on. Where do you want to go?"

"It doesn't matter. Maybe someplace with a drive-thru. That way we won't have to get out."

"The place in the business loop makes good coffee."

"Fine."

He followed her outside. "I'll drive." He pulled open the passenger door on the company truck.

"Thanks." She climbed in as he moseyed to the driver's side. Not that he knew Sierra well, but he could tell she either didn't want to be around people, or she didn't want to get stuck inside a coffee shop and forced to sit and talk—perhaps, too much like a date. Probably the latter. He cranked the key and pulled out. "Other than the plumbing issue, the house is coming along nicely."

"I noticed."

"Really? You were hardly in the frame of mind—"

"How do you know my frame of mind?" she snapped. "Sorry. That was uncalled for. I need to stop snapping at people. Just so you know, I'm not normally like this. I had a rough night and didn't sleep well, but it's no excuse."

His stomach churned. "Spencer didn't do anything to cause that rough night did he?" From what he'd seen of the cop, Spencer seemed like a stand-up guy, but if he was giving Sierra a hard time, he'd have a talk with the man and put a stop to it immediately—cop or not.

"Not directly, no." She sighed. "As a disinterested third party, maybe you can help me."

He gripped the steering wheel. Sierra must be really

upset about something if she was willing to talk about personal issues.

"My son is fifteen, and he wants to meet his birth father."

He didn't know his dad? Why not? Wait, he didn't even know she had a son. No way could he ask all the questions racing through his mind. She'd shut down for sure, and he'd like to help her if he could.

"The thing is, I don't know if I want him back in our lives. He gave up his parental rights and left when Trey was only a year old. It's been just the two of us ever since. The idea of allowing him any contact with my son makes me want to go crazy with a staple gun. Seriously though, why would Trey want to meet his dad? Aren't I enough?"

"Whoa. You *are* having a rough time of it." He pulled up to the coffee window and ordered a mocha for him and a chai for her. This conversation would take longer than their treats would last. They stayed silent while waiting for their drinks. After paying, he pulled out. "Do you mind if we take the scenic route back? I want to check out some property I heard about."

"That's fine." She sipped the tea. "By the way. Thanks. I needed to vent to someone who wouldn't care a whit about me and my son."

"What makes you think I don't care?"

"How could you? You don't know me."

He shrugged. "Not well, but I can't see how that matters. I'd like to get to know you."

Her soft gasp joined the hum of road noise. "Thanks. Now that you mention it, I'd like for us to know one another better too. It will make working together easier if you know how I think."

Ha. Like that could ever happen. But he wasn't about to tell her that. "So you're upset that your son suddenly wants his dad in his life. Any idea what brought this on?"

She crossed an arm over her middle. "None. There've been some changes recently. We moved to Sunriver for starters. When we were moving in, we triggered the silent alarm. This is what I was going to tell you about the other day and never got to it. Spencer is the cop that responded to the alarm. He thought we were robbing the place, and by the time I got outside to see what all the ruckus was about, he had my son face down on the driveway with a gun pointed at him."

He whistled low and slow. "I'm no psychologist, but I think that's your trigger event. He probably needs a man to talk to about guy stuff."

She shook her head. "Oh. No. He does not want *a* man. He wants his dad. And for the life of me I don't know why. If any man would work, I'd let you have a whirl at him." She chuckled. "That did not sound right."

He grinned. "I got the point. I guess you'd better figure out why he wants his dad before you move forward. Maybe he only thinks he wants his dad, but what he really wants is a male father figure." Oh boy, now *he'd* put his foot in it.

"That's not happening. When he thought Spencer wanted to date me, he told him I don't date and was very rude to him, so I don't think just any man would work."

"I see. Well, maybe you should at least rule that out. Since we work together, and I'm not a cop, maybe I could stop by sometime and we could shoot hoops or something. What does your son enjoy?"

"He's a runner."

"No kidding. I run too. What about you?"

"Only if necessary. I have no idea where his running bug came from. Do you really think he only needs to have a man to talk to?"

"I don't know your son, but it's possible."

"I sure like the idea of him running with you over him meeting his dad."

He tuned in to what she wasn't saying. "Is there a problem with his dad?"

She shrugged.

He slowed as he approached the lot he was interested in building on, then pulled to the side of the road and put the pickup in park. Too bad the property wasn't further away. They needed more time to talk, but it would have to wait for now.

"What are we doing?" Her voice trembled slightly.

She didn't trust him? Or maybe it was men in general that made her nervous. "This is the property I wanted to see. Do you mind if I get out and walk it?"

Her face relaxed. "Not at all. I'll join you." She met him at the hood. "Is this a new Belafonte property?"

"No. I'm considering buying it for myself. I'd like to have a house of my own."

"You don't have one?"

"I live in a studio apartment. It's time for a change."

"Going from a studio to a house will certainly be a change."

"Mmm-hmm." He liked the property and the location. It wasn't a huge lot, but it fit his budget, and he had confidence that Stephen would design the perfect house for the land. He suddenly realized how quiet they had gotten. He looked at Sierra who seemed preoccupied with something on the edge of the property line. "What is it?"

She turned with a finger to her lips.

He moved to her side and saw what had grabbed her attention—a coyote. "I'm not a big fan of those guys."

"But he's fascinating to watch. Look, I think he has something in his sights."

"So long as it's not a kid. They're not above attacking a small child if no adults are around." The nearest house was one lot away, and it looked unoccupied. He breathed easier. "You ready to go?"

She turned toward him. "Sure. Time to go back to reality."

He chuckled and dropped his hand onto her shoulder. "It can't be that bad." He was glad she didn't shrug off his hand, but he removed it nonetheless. They went back to where he'd parked and hopped in. He did a U-turn toward Spencer's house.

She shifted in her seat. "I've been thinking about what you said about running with Trey. What if I decide to join him and invite you along?"

He shook his head. "He's not going to talk in front of you."

"I get that, but it would give you an opportunity to meet him. If the two of you hit it off, you could run together again without me."

He glanced her way. "I thought you didn't run."

"I'm willing to make an exception in this case." She laid out a plan for when and where they could *accidentally* meet.

Getting involved in Sierra's personal life might not be a good idea, considering she made it clear she wasn't interested in him. He wasn't out to get hurt, but friends helped friends, and he felt for her son and wanted to help. This seemed like an innocent enough plan to see if he could assist the teen. "Okay. I'm in. I know the place you're talking about. I'll meet you there."

"Thanks."

"Any idea what you're going to do about your son's dad?"

"Not a clue. I'd like to test your theory about Trey only wanting to have a man to talk to. Until yesterday I had no idea if Randy was dead or alive. Spencer located him a lot faster than I expected."

John's dad died several years ago. There were times when he craved a father figure, and *he* was in his thirties. He could only imagine how a teenager would feel. "Your plan is solid. I'll let you know my take on things with Trey."

"Thanks." Surprise filled her voice. "I appreciate it."

There was a lot more to Sierra than he'd at first realized. Maybe that line she'd drawn wasn't as firm as he'd thought.

CHAPTER TEN

SIERRA SAT AT THE DINING ROOM table staring at the computer screen. She folded her hands in her lap. Spencer had sent over everything he had on Randy including a recent photo. He sported a close shaved beard and looked well kept. She looked closer and gasped. Trey looked exactly like Randy. How had she not noticed before? They had the same eyes, mouth, even their smile was the same.

"Who's that?"

Sierra jumped and slapped the screen closed. "Trey, I didn't hear you come up behind me."

"You were pretty intense. Who's the man on the screen?"

"No one."

Trey pulled out a chair and sat. "You've always told me you don't tolerate lies. He's someone or you wouldn't have been looking at him like that."

Sierra's heart raced. She wasn't ready to have this conversation, but it seemed she was stuck. She sighed. "He's your dad."

Trey stood almost tipping the chair in the process. "For real? Let me see him again."

"Are you sure you want to see him?"

"His picture, yes. Him? Maybe, maybe not. I don't know anymore. It's not like he cared enough about me to stick around and be my dad, so I'm not sure I care to be his son."

Her gaze met his. Hurt and a spark of anger lit his eyes. She needed to defuse this somehow. But right now, showing him Randy's picture would have to do. She lifted the top and pulled up the photo again. She watched her son stare unsmiling at the screen.

"Do you think I look like him?"

The spitting image. "You have his nose, eyes, and smile."

Trey nodded. "Yeah. I see that now. I wish I didn't look like him."

"Why's that?"

He shrugged. "Just do. I'm headed out for a run."

"Hold up. I'll join you."

He froze. "You're kidding? You. Don't. Run." He looked at her as if she'd lost her mind.

"I've put on a little weight since I've started drinking so many chai teas. Can't a mom try something new?"

He crossed his arms and chuckled. "Whatever. But hurry. I'll meet you out front."

Sierra turned her head to hide her smile. Trey almost always ran about now, and she had it worked out with John to meet them on a nearby path in ten minutes. Would they be too early? She didn't want to miss him. She changed into spandex and a long shirt, pulled on the running shoes she'd picked up on a recent trip to Bend, then headed outside. She rubbed her arms. "There's a nip in the air. I'll go grab a sweatshirt."

Trey rolled his eyes. "You'll be fine. Come on."

"Okay. Okay. Please start slow. I don't want to die in the first five minutes."

He chuckled. "I'll take it easy on you."

"We never talked about Spencer. Did you work on forgiving him?" This running thing was harder than she realized. They'd only been running a minute or two and she already wanted to stop.

"Yeah. I did, but I still don't like him." He kicked up his pace.

Sierra's stomach plummeted. That was not what she wanted to hear. She struggled to keep up. "Hey," she panted. "This . . . is not . . . easy." She'd never make it to the rendezvous point at this pace. Her calves already hurt.

A runner came up beside her. "Hey, Sierra. Looks like you could use a break." John flashed white teeth.

"I'm good." *Not!*

Trey looked over his shoulder. "You know each other?"

Thankfully John responded because she could barely breathe much less carry on a conversation.

"I work with your mom."

"You're an interior designer?" Trey scrunched his nose.

"Ha! No. I'm in charge of the worksite."

"I'm done." Sierra slowed to a walk.

"Want me to stop, Mom?" Trey turned and jogged in place.

She waved them on. "Run with John. I'm too out of shape to keep up."

"We'll catch you on the way back," John said.

As much as she wanted to keep pace with them, there was no way. Maybe she should head to the house. No, she'd been serious about gaining a little weight. If she was going to indulge in a sugary drink she needed to up her activity. She stopped to stretch then started at a slow jog.

Much better. Her son had no idea what going slow meant.

She'd give anything to be a mosquito on John or Trey's shoulders. What would they talk about? Would they talk? Yes, John always managed to draw her into conversation, even when she was determined to stay quiet. He had a gift.

John kept stride with Trey. The teen had good form. They ran in silence for probably a mile. Somehow he had to get the teen to start talking. "How long have you been a runner?"

"I've always liked running. I used to spend my recesses running the track rather than playing." Trey slid a glance at him. "So you work with my mom. That means you know the cop."

"If you mean Spencer, yes, I do. I take it from your tone, you don't care for him."

"I can't stand him. I don't know how the two of you can work at his place. My mom actually went to church with him."

"She mentioned how you met. That would have shaken me up to say the least." He wasn't sure what to expect from Sierra's son, but his boldness and hostility toward Spencer surprised him a little, even though he'd been given a heads-up about what had happened.

"Really?"

"For sure. No one wants a gun pointed at him. Especially when you have no idea why."

"Exactly!"

"Did he apologize?"

"Yeah, sort of. He said he was doing his job, and had no way of knowing we weren't robbing the place. It was clear he felt bad about what happened."

John glanced at the teen and noted the perplexed look on his face. "That sounds like Spencer. From what I've seen, he's a stand up guy."

Trey grunted. "I should probably turn around and head back to my mom. She never runs and we kind of left her in our dust."

John chuckled. "I'll head back too."

"You sure?"

"Yeah."

"You like my mom, don't you?"

He chuckled. "I do. Is that okay? We don't know each other well, but I hope that will change over time. Although I hear she doesn't date, so we're just friends."

"True, but you seem alright. She likes M & Ms."

"Thanks." This kid cracked him up, but no way would he laugh and risk alienating him. He was smart enough to know if Trey approved of him, he'd have a better chance with Sierra—but was it a good idea considering the signals she'd sent? He'd determined to back off, but the more he got to know her the more he regretted that decision. It wouldn't hurt to revisit the idea. The woman had some serious walls, but in spite of everything he hoped to be able to scale them with the help of her son.

They ran side by side in silence for a good distance before spotting Sierra jogging at a slow but steady pace toward them. She waved when she spotted them, then turned in the opposite direction, probably hoping for a head start. Unless they slowed to a walk they'd bypass her within seconds. "I'll walk with your mom back to the house if that's okay with you."

Trey nodded and zipped past his mom. "See ya!"

John eased up beside her and slowed to a fast walk. "He's a great kid."

"Thanks. How'd it go?"

"Well, I think. He mentioned his issue with Spencer. His dad never came up."

"I didn't expect he would. Trey saw a picture of him earlier, and I'm not sure, but I think he might want to pass on meeting him. He said, and I quote: 'It's not like he cared enough about me to stick around and be my dad, so I'm not sure I care to be his son.'"

"Ouch." He hurt for the teen. His own dad had been great, and he couldn't imagine not having had him in his life. "Are you going to make jogging a regular thing?"

"I'm considering it—at least for a little while. I need to connect with Trey somehow, and no matter how much I hate to run, this seems to be the best way. I think if you hadn't showed up he would have slowed and kept pace with me eventually."

"You might be right." The house loomed ahead. Disappointment shot through him. He wanted to continue their conversation.

"Would you like to come in for a glass of water?"

"That'd be great. Thanks." *Score!* He had a bottle of water in his Jeep parked at the end of the cul-de-sac but much preferred to take her up on her offer. He'd been a little late and had rushed without properly hydrating beforehand.

Sierra slowed to a walk then stopped in the driveway. She stretched one leg back then the other.

John took the opportunity to stretch as well. A couple of minutes later Sierra led the way inside.

"We're back, Trey," she said.

Though not his taste, the house was very nice. His mom would approve for sure. "How did you meet the owner of this place?"

"Mrs. Drake was a client."

He frowned. "That's right." He would never forget this homeowner. She had been demanding from day one. So much so that he'd requested before and after pictures to include in her file, just in case she chose to cause problems later. "She was a challenge."

"I keep hearing that about her, but she's been a gem to me," Sierra said as she led the way into the kitchen. "How is it you know her? I thought you only work with the construction side of the business."

"Although the design and construction businesses are separate, when there is a problem with anything, I'm the one to take care of it. It didn't use to be that way, but now that my mom has retired, Stephen asked me to take on the role."

Sierra pulled two glasses from the cupboard then filled them with tap water. "I don't recall there being any issues with this project. It went very smoothly."

"Good. That means I did my job well. She was a handful, and Bailey sent her my way before the project started which was good, since Mrs. Drake refused to pay her bill. She said the cost was higher than she expected and the work wasn't up to her standards."

"You're kidding." She handed him a glass. "Everything, including the price, was laid out in the contract before work began. She told me she loved what we did."

"After I brought the contract to her attention she paid the bill in full and dropped the issue." It helped that he had before and after pictures too, to remind her exactly what had been done.

"I'm beginning to think Mrs. Drake has a split personality. Spencer mentioned something about her as well."

"She has a reputation for being difficult." He raised the glass to his lips.

Sierra chuckled. "Funny, I believe that was the word Spencer used to describe her too. I'm glad she likes me. We've gotten along quite well."

"Count yourself fortunate." He set the glass on the counter. "I should go." He didn't want to give her a reason to put her walls back in place by overstaying his welcome. "Can you stop by Spencer's sometime tomorrow?"

"Sure. Is there a problem?"

"Maybe. The bathroom tile isn't the right size, and I need to know if you want to use it or not."

"Are you serious? This is the second time that's happened. It's as if someone is trying to sabotage me."

"More like Belafonte Design. I take it Bailey hasn't said anything?"

She shook her head. "I'm not sure what you're talking about."

Maybe he shouldn't have opened his mouth, but she had a right to know. "Someone has been calling and changing orders with our vendors. At first we thought it was a simple clerical error, but I dug deeper, and it appears someone called claiming to represent us." He was relieved to learn it wasn't his mother, but the alternative was worse. Someone seemed to have declared war on the Belafontes, and he had no idea why.

Shock covered her face. He was glad, too, because Rick had suggested Sierra was the troublemaker, since all this began about the time she was hired. He had already ruled her out after the plumbing issue, but it was a relief to see with his own eyes that this was the first she knew of any issues. "I can see you're astonished."

"I am. I don't understand why someone would do this. What will they gain by messing up our orders?"

"If they want to discredit us with our clients they are doing a great job. Thankfully we have a stellar reputation, but if much more of this happens word is going to spread, and we will begin to lose business."

"Maybe Spencer can help. Has this been reported to the police?"

He shook his head. "I'm not sure we have a case."

"Whoever is doing this must be breaking some law. We need to tell him, at least to see if he can help. In the meantime, have you let our vendors know what's going on so that they won't continue to be duped?"

"Well, no. I was really hoping to keep this on the down low."

"Not a good idea." Sierra shook her head. "One of us needs to go in person to each of the vendors and tell them they must ask to see identification if there's an order change. It's a pain, but this has to stop. Time is money and receiving the wrong materials costs us and makes us look bad to our clients."

"Okay. I see your point. I'll get on that too— tomorrow. Tonight I have a date with a hot tub."

She chuckled. "That sounds nice. I can't believe Mrs.

Drake doesn't have a hot tub."

"They're not for everyone. Okay, I'm out. See you tomorrow." He saw himself to the door and headed to his Jeep a little ways up the street. Two deer meandered across the road to the center island covered in grasses and trees. Their calming presence was always welcome, and he never tired of seeing the deer. Especially after talking about whomever was trying to sabotage their company. The thing that confused him the most was that the caller always claimed to be Mona, but his mom denied calling businesses and changing orders. Was Mom trying to hold onto one last shred of authority? But if that was the case, wouldn't she own up to it?

CHAPTER ELEVEN

THE FOLLOWING EVENING SIERRA EASED ONTO a bench in the Sunriver Village beside Spencer. "Thanks for meeting me here."

"Sure. What's up? You sounded so mysterious on the phone." He quirked a grin.

"Sorry. There were people around and this needs to stay quiet."

Concern filled his eyes. "Does this have something to do with Randy?"

"No. Although, I have spoken with Trey, and he's not sure he wants to meet his dad after all. I dodged that bullet."

He frowned.

"Sorry. That was in poor humor."

He shrugged. "So why am I here?"

She glanced over her shoulder to make sure no one lingered close enough to hear their conversation. "Someone is trying to sabotage the Belafontes."

John had said to not go to Spencer for help, but she knew if anyone could help it was him. If she'd learned anything over the past weeks it was that Spencer was a good man and a good cop. He could be trusted.

"What do you mean?"

"Remember the broken water pipe at your house?"

"How could I forget?"

"Deliberate. Someone is also calling our suppliers and changing or cancelling orders. There has been vandalism at construction sites as well, dating back as far as November."

"I heard about one incident, but why didn't anyone report the rest?" Frustration filled his tone.

"They didn't want to lose business. People are less likely to hire a company riddled with problems, according to John."

"He's probably right. I'll do what I can, but if anything more happens, promise me you will file a police report."

She hesitated. John would not be happy if he found out she'd gone to Spencer, and he would be furious if she filed a police report.

"What?"

"The family doesn't want to involve the police. They filed one when some equipment was damaged, but nothing came of it. They don't see the point and feel it could do more harm than good."

"Then what are you expecting me to do?"

"I don't know. Camp out at one of the sites and wait for trouble?" Okay, so that sounded better in her head than it did when she said it aloud.

"I suppose I could." Something sparked in his eye. "What's in it for me?"

Hope filled her. "What do you have in mind?"

"How about you help me organize the mentor program."

"What are you talking about?" She'd thought to toss a few sporting event or concert tickets his way, not tie up more of her personal time.

"Ever since the incident with your son, I've been

trying to come up with a way to show him and others that police are the good guys. We care about them and our community. We want to serve and protect them. I thought if the department had a mentor program it would go a long way in showing local kids that cops are people, too, with families and a life outside of their job."

Her heart warmed at his thoughtfulness and passion for others. There was a lot more to Spencer than she'd realized. Suddenly, giving up a little personal time didn't bother her in the slightest. "That's a wonderful idea. I would love to help you. Do we have a deal then?"

This had worked out well. She loved doing community service and at the same time she'd be helping the Belafontes. It was a win-win for everyone.

"Almost. I want to be Trey's mentor."

She shook her head and her stomach sank. "Excuse me?"

"I know you heard me." He shot her a teasing grin.

"I did, but why would you want to be my son's mentor? He's come a long way since that day, but I don't think he will ever like you."

He winced.

"Sorry. But I don't believe in sugar coating things."

"I think I can change his mind about me if we spend time together doing things he enjoys."

Her shoulders tensed. Talk about feeling torn. "Tell you what. I will agree to make sure he is signed up for the program and that he takes part for at least three months. The rest is up to you."

"Deal!" He thrust out his hand.

She grasped it and a jolt shot up her arm. What was that all about? She quickly stood. "I should go."

"Why the hurry? I was hoping to get more information on my mission." He waggled his brow.

She chuckled. His playful side surprised her. "Umm. Well . . . I don't really know much more."

"You're going to have to do better if you want help."

"Okay. Give me a few days to see what specifics I can dig up." Maybe she should bring Bailey in on this. "Hey, are you and Bailey good friends? I imagine she'd have more information than me and could help."

"I wouldn't call us close, but yes, we're friends. If you feel like you can go to her with this, then please do. She's tight with a buddy of mine's wife. Mark is an excellent detective and if anyone can figure this out it's him. If you don't mind, I'd like to bring him in on this once it's official."

"I don't mind, but I still have to figure out how to *make* it official without getting fired."

"Good luck with that." He stood. "I hear my house is going to be finished soon."

She stood and walked with him toward the parking lot. "Yes. I'll be there tomorrow to take care of the finishing touches." She owed this man a lot for all he'd done for her and here she was asking for more. "Would you like to come over for dinner sometime?"

"I thought I was public enemy number one."

She laughed. "I wouldn't go that far. Besides, if you want to mentor my son . . ."

"I'll be there." He stopped beside her SUV.

"Text me the details."

She quirked a grin. "Will do." With a little extra bounce in her step she hopped into her vehicle.

The following morning Sierra sat across from Bailey at the office in Mona's house. "There's something I need to tell you."

Bailey closed her laptop. "This sounds serious. Is everything okay?"

She shook her head. "Not really, but this shouldn't be news to you." She went on to lay out her plan regarding bringing in Spencer to help figure out who was trying to harm the Belafontes' company. "He needs us to file a police report whenever anything happens. He knows about the one Mark has."

"Mark is a friend. I bet he'd help in an unofficial capacity if we asked."

"Probably. But why should he have to if all we need to do is file another police report?"

Bailey pressed her lips together and tapped her fingers on the desk. "You're right, but I'm not sure. I don't want to upset anyone. Maybe I should run this by Stephen."

Her stomach jolted. "If he knows what we want to do, won't he stop us?" Telling Stephen could ruin everything.

"It's all in the delivery. I have an idea that might work and make everyone happy." For the next thirty minutes Bailey laid out a convoluted plan on how to get everyone together.

"I like it. I'll host the dinner at my house. You'll take care to make sure Mark and Nicole will be there?"

"Yes. I think I'll invite John and Sarah too."

"Sarah?"

"She's another friend. I trust her, and the more this appears to be a party, the less suspicion we'll draw from Stephen and John. We need them to show up, or this will be for nothing."

"Won't they mind being put on the spot?"

"Maybe, but I don't think they'll get angry and try to stop us once it's out there and others know. They'll want to let the guys get to the bottom of it. If I know Mark and Spencer like I think I do, then they will be able to persuade Stephen and John to let them investigate."

"I sure hope you're right because I don't want to lose my job over this."

Bailey's face turned even more serious. "I understand that fear, but you should know, I have only heard good things about your work at Spencer's, and one of our most difficult clients adores you, so I wouldn't worry too much."

"Thanks. I keep hearing about Mrs. Drake from others. It's like she's a Jekyll and Hyde." She stood and grabbed her bag. "I'll be at Spencer's if you need me." Even though everything seemed to be going right, her stomach said otherwise.

Spencer took the keys John held out to him. "Thanks. My place looks great."

"I'm glad you like it. I'm surprised Sierra isn't here. My mom always liked to walk through with the owners as she showed off her masterpieces."

The door burst open, and Sierra rushed in. "Sorry I'm

late. I can't believe I missed the big reveal. I had to run to Bend, and traffic slowed me down."

Spencer chuckled. "I've been living here while construction is going on, so the final product is not a big surprise."

"I know, but I still . . ."

"Maybe you'd like to walk through with me now?"

A smile lit her eyes but only for a moment.

"Yes. Thank you." She strolled beside him asking how he liked this and that, but all he could manage was a nod or a grunt. Something was off with Sierra. What had happened since they'd last spoken?

John followed after them. "It looks like you have this under control, Sierra. I'm going to head out now."

She glanced over her shoulder. "Sounds good. 'Bye."

The door clicked closed, and she blew out a breath. "I'm so glad he's gone."

He raised a brow. "Why?"

"I have news."

His senses kicked into work mode. "Okay. What's up?"

"Remember when I asked you over for dinner?"

He nodded. What did that have to do with the sabotage?

"Well, I decided to talk with Bailey about things, and she came up with a great plan."

He listened as she laid out her idea. Although the plan could work, he didn't like putting John and his brother on the spot like that. He sure wouldn't want anyone to do that to him. Plus, he was giving up what he'd hoped would be a romantic dinner at her place. But Sierra's enthusiasm was palpable, and he wouldn't disappoint her by stomping down her idea.

"Well? What do you think?"

"I think you and Bailey have your minds made up, and what I think matters little." He grinned hoping to soften his words, even if they were true.

"Do you mind sharing your dinner with a crowd?"

"What if I say yes?"

The look of shock on her face was priceless. He stifled a chuckle and tried to remain stoic.

Her eyes widened. "Then I'd reschedule our dinner for another time."

He guided them toward the living room and sat. A smile escaped. "I would enjoy keeping our original plan, *and* I will go along with your scheme."

She blew out a breath as if she'd been holding it. "Thank you!" She hugged him, taking them both by surprise if her suddenly pink cheeks meant anything. "Sorry. Sometimes I act before thinking."

He chuckled. "We're all guilty of that from time to time. I suppose congratulations are in order."

"For what?"

"A job well done. In spite of the problems, I like how everything turned out. And you came in under budget. Great job."

"Thanks!" She stood. "I'll get out of your hair."

"You don't have to leave."

"I should go anyway. I have a party to plan and a couple of menus to come up with."

"You don't have to make anything fancy for our dinner. I'll bring Chinese."

She crossed her arms. "No. Having you bring the meal kind of defeats the purpose. Don't you think? But that wouldn't stop *me* from picking up takeout." She flashed him a grin before heading toward the door. She spun around and faced him. "When we first met, I never would have predicted we'd be friends."

His insides warmed. "I'd have to agree. I'm pleased to count you as a friend." He'd like for them to be more, but now was not the time to go there.

CHAPTER TWELVE

FRIDAY MORNING SPENCER TYPED UP A proposal for the mentor program to give to the captain. Now that he had Mark and Sierra on board, he felt comfortable trying to make it official. A couple of firefighters at the station next door were interested, as well. Who would have thought a silent alarm call would have led to this?

His phone rang. "Spencer speaking."

"Hi. It's Sierra. There's been another incident."

"Are you filing an official police report?"

"Yes. Bailey is onboard. It happened at the project she's working on. The owners are beside themselves, and if they haven't called the police already, they will soon."

"Are you sure this has anything to do with Belafonte Design?" It sounded like it might be a random act.

"Yes. Whoever did it spray painted a message on the homeowners' living room wall, and it was directed at us."

He grabbed a pen and pulled out his notepad. "This changes things." He wrote down the address. "Okay. I'm not working today, but I'll check into this. Thanks for the call."

"Sure. Will you keep me in the loop?" Her voice sounded weary and scared at the same time.

"As much as I can. Try and not worry, Sierra. Whoever this is sounds like they have an issue with the Belafontes, not you."

"I know, but that still worries me. I care about this company and these people. I don't want to see them hurt."

"Understood. I'll let you know what I find out. Is the party still on for tonight?"

"Yes. Assuming everyone is still coming. Although there's really no need now that this has happened."

"You can't cancel now." He wanted to see with his own eyes that she was okay.

"I won't. See you later."

"'Bye." He placed his phone on the table and saved what he'd been working on. He wasn't scheduled to work today, but Mark was, and he had probably been the officer sent to process the scene because of his background as a detective.

Spencer hit his buddy's number on the contact screen and waited.

"Hey, Spencer."

"I got a call from Sierra this morning. What do you have?"

"No leads, but whoever did this wanted to send a message. They aim to put the Belafontes out of business."

"Any idea why?"

"Not yet."

"Did the homeowner have video surveillance?"

"Yes, but the perp wore all black from head to toe. The only thing we can glean from the video is that it appears to be a woman or maybe a slight male between five-feet-five inches and five-eight. I'm leaning toward it being a woman."

"That's more than they knew before. Interesting. Did she take anything?"

"No. What stumps me is how she knew the Belafontes

were working there. It was only directed at them. So why not spray paint Mona's house or the office in Bend?"

"Maybe they were afraid of being recognized."

"Dressed in all black?"

"Be sure to show everyone associated with their business the video. I suspect they know this person."

"Already on it. I'm bringing it to the party tonight."

Sounds like tonight wouldn't be much of a party after all. He felt bad about that for Bailey's sake. Then again the point of tonight had been to bring up the problem. At least now they'd no longer be springing anything on Stephen and John. "Maybe the brothers could meet up at the station beforehand so the other guests don't see the video."

"That would be best. I was trying to make it easier on everyone, though. I'll see what I can arrange."

Spencer pocketed his phone. The Bible he'd purchased after attending the prophecy talk caught his eye. He'd read and reread all the verses the speaker had listed which had made him want to read more of the big book. The Bible intrigued him, although he didn't understand everything in it. He was constantly drawn to its pages. He wanted what Mark and Sierra had. He saw peace in them, even when things weren't going the way they desired. He needed that too. He'd had an appointment with the pastor earlier today at the church he'd visited and had been surprised when he'd given him a card entitled 'The Sinners Prayer.' Everything the pastor said made sense, but could it really be that easy?

He prayed the prayer with the pastor, but was that seriously all there was to being a Christian? Mark would happily answer any questions he had, but he was a little embarrassed by his ignorance. Would Sierra welcome his questions? Hadn't she said as much?

He would love to discuss his newfound faith with her, but it felt so personal. Would she think he'd overstepped the boundaries she'd set? She'd made no secret of her desire to stay single. Not that answering Bible questions was romantic, but it would thrust them together more. He liked that idea, but wouldn't use his ignorance or newfound faith as a device to get a woman.

Even though he had the day off, he couldn't sit and ponder this. He had things to do. Finishing his proposal for the mentor program was at the top of his list.

For the next hour he outlined his plan. Finally satisfied, he emailed it to the captain. The rest was up to his boss.

Sierra added tomatoes to the top of the salad. "Trey, our guests will be here any minute. Will you make sure your bathroom is neat and tidy?"

She'd cleaned it earlier, but having him stand around doing nothing put her on edge.

The doorbell pealed.

"I'll get it," Trey hollered as he darted to the door.

Sierra rinsed her hands then followed after him. "Welcome. Trey, you know my boss Bailey, and this is Stephen, her boyfriend."

Trey shook Stephen's hand. "I met your brother John the other evening."

"Oh?" he asked.

"Yeah. We met on the trail, running."

It sounded like John had made a good impression on her son. Maybe all Trey had wanted was a male in his life after all. It would be a relief to not have to deal with Randy. Trey hadn't brought his father up since the other night, and she hoped the matter was dropped for good.

She spotted Spencer, Sarah, Nicole, and Mark on the porch through the window and pulled open the door. "I'm glad you could all make it." She stepped aside, allowing them to enter. "The lasagna will be ready soon. It looks like the only person we're waiting on is John."

Stephen nodded. "My brother had to deal with something and will be a little late. He said not to wait."

Disappointment shot through her. "I hope everything is okay?"

"There's nothing to worry about," Stephen said. "Our mom's caregiver was running late."

"Oh. I see." Was that really what kept him, or had there been a lead in finding out who had targeted the Belafontes, and that was what kept him? No. The men would have said something. She had it on good authority that Mark was the lead investigator on the case. She tried to shake off her disappointment and focus on the guests that were here.

They filtered into the kitchen, dining, and living rooms. The ladies joined her in the kitchen. "Thanks for letting me leave early, Bailey. I never would have been able to pull this off otherwise."

"It wasn't a problem. After what happened earlier, I wasn't in a frame of mind to work, either. I ended up going home, too."

Relief washed over her. "Oh good. I was afraid I'd left you in the lurch."

"Not at all."

"Is there anything we can help you with?" Nicole asked. Nicole and Sarah were good friends, and from what she'd observed, they'd embraced Bailey as a friend. It seemed the three of them hung out together a lot.

"Everything is pretty much done, but maybe you could put ice in the glasses?" She pointed to the glasses lined up on the counter. "We use the icemaker in the door. The water spigot is broken, so tap water will have to do."

"Will do." Nicole got to work.

The other ladies pitched in, and soon they had everything on the counter buffet style. A knock sounded on the door, then it swung open.

John walked in. "Sorry I'm late." His gaze found Sierra's.

Her insides warmed. "No problem. Dinner is just now ready." She was happy he'd made it. At least now her son would have someone he felt comfortable visiting with.

Spencer sidled up to her. "Trey looks like he hates me a little less than the last time I saw him."

She almost laughed but held it in, unwilling to answer the questions her outburst would surely bring. "Baby steps." She patted his arm. "Okay, everyone. You can sit at any spot at the table. There's bread, lasagna, salad, and dressing on the island and drinks by the fridge." She offered a blessing for the food. "Amen. Enjoy!" She meandered to the end of the line and stood behind her son, who knew they always let their guests go first.

He spoke softly out the side of his mouth. "Why'd you invite Spencer?"

"He's a friend, and he's helping me with something."

Trey frowned. "You like him." It wasn't a question.

She hesitated. Her feelings for Spencer had been rapidly changing. Could her son handle the truth? She looked him in the eye—yes, he might hold a grudge, but she had no doubt of her son's love for her. She could be honest. "I do. He's a nice man. And he's been there for me several times since I've met him. People like that are hard to come by. I wish you—"

"I know, Mom. I'm trying. He's not a bad guy. But every time I see him I remember what happened."

She rubbed his arm. "I'm sorry about that. I blame myself. If I'd turned off the alarm it never would have happened."

Trey raised a brow and quirked a grin. "True. I think you owe me."

She playfully punched his shoulder. The line moved quickly, and they were soon all seated around Mrs. Drake's huge dining room table.

John cleared his throat. "I'm glad you're all here tonight. This worked out well. I hope you ladies don't mind me bringing up a work situation." He addressed Nicole and Sarah.

"No." They said in unison.

"Thanks. By now everyone has heard about the vandalism that took place at a client's house. I spent much of the day trying to figure out who could be targeting us, and I've come up with a short list. Do any of you have someone to add?" He read off three names—one she recognized as a former client and the others were a mystery to her.

Sierra shook her head. "I can't think of any disgruntled clients."

Stephen rubbed his chin. "Dad had a nemesis once

upon a time."

"Go on," Spencer said.

"It was a long time ago. The guy was younger than Dad, and I remember Dad calling him a go-getter. They often bid on the same jobs, but Dad was more established. I think the man left town."

"Then why bring it up?" Mark asked.

"Because this is the kind of thing he'd do. He was furious Dad won a bid that he was desperate to get. Apparently his business was on the brink of bankruptcy, and he needed that job to stay solvent."

John nodded. "I remember now. The guy was kind of scary. Dad told us to call 911 if he ever approached us."

Spencer raised a brow. "Sounds worth checking out to me. What's his name?"

"Davis," John said. He looked to Stephen. "Do you remember the rest of his name?"

He shook his head. "Dad only called him Davis."

Mark tapped a finger on the table. "What about your mom? Would she know?"

"Maybe," Stephen said. "I can ask her later. I've been thinking about who it could be all day, and I can't even come up with a disgruntled former client."

"It doesn't have to be a disgruntled client," Spencer said. "What about a former employee?"

"Rick fired a gal and her boyfriend last fall for smoking pot on the job," John said.

"Get me their contact info, and I'll look into their alibis," Mark said.

"Sure."

"Speaking of old employees," Stephen said. "I saw a woman we interviewed to be Bailey's assistant in the village today. Apparently she found a job working for a new interior design company here in Sunriver."

"What about the conversation concerned you?" Spencer asked.

"Nothing really. Your question made me remember. I always like to see people succeed. It was nice to know she landed on her feet."

"I'm glad she found another job." Bailey reached for her water goblet. "She looked great on paper, but in person she was like a whirlwind."

Mark chuckled. "I'll check her out too," Mark said. "What's her name?"

"Celia something." Stephen pulled out his smart phone. He ran his fingers over it for a few seconds then frowned. "I thought I might have her info on my phone, but I guess not. I'll have to look at her resume for her last name and contact info. But I don't think it's necessary to waste your time looking into her. She seemed quite happy."

"Nonetheless, will one of you text her contact info to me later?" Mark asked.

John glanced at Bailey who looked like she'd eaten something rotten. "Can you get that to him?"

"I didn't save it. When we hired Sierra, I shredded Celia's information."

Relief washed over Sierra. The family was finally taking the threat seriously and doing something about whoever was targeting them. Hopefully, Spencer and Mark would solve this mystery sooner than later.

The house phone rang. "Please excuse me." Sierra stood and reached for the house phone. "Hello?"

"Sierra, dear. How are things going?" Mrs. Drake

asked.

"Fine. Your home is lovely. My son and I are enjoying our time here. How's your vacation?" Laughter erupted from the direction of the dining room. She took the cordless as far away from the group as possible.

"Do you have guests?" An accusatory tone filled Mrs. Drake's voice. But why? It wasn't as if she said no one else was allowed into her home.

"Yes. I'm having a dinner party."

"How nice." Syrup dripped from her voice.

An uneasy feeling gripped Sierra's stomach.

"The reason I'm calling is to let you know that I will be returning sooner than I'd planned."

Sierra's pulse accelerated. "Oh. When?"

"One month. I have a business interest in Sunriver that needs my attention."

How was she supposed to uproot her son again in such a short amount of time? It wasn't fair. "But you were supposed to be gone a year." She heard the panic in her voice. She took a calming breath.

"Plans change. Anyhoo, I need you to vacate in three weeks."

"But I thought you said a month."

"Yes, dear. But I'm having the house cleaned from top to bottom before I arrive, and I want it spotless when I get there. Toodles."

The line went dead. Of all the rotten things to do. She headed back to her guests who suddenly grew silent.

"What's wrong?" Spencer asked.

"That was Mrs. Drake. She's coming back early. We have to be out in three weeks." What was she going to do?

John sat on the sofa in Sierra's living room, his hands fisted at his sides. It seemed one bad thing after another kept happening. His mom's health was not improving, the business was being threatened by some wacko, and now Mrs. Drake was kicking Sierra out. When would it all stop?

Sierra stood in the kitchen talking with Spencer. He wondered at the two of them. She claimed to not date, but when he watched them together there seemed to be a spark of something. If that was the case, he wished them both the best. As much as he'd hoped to be the one where Spencer stood, he got it—she wasn't interested in him in that way. But they were well on their way to a solid friendship, and he would take all the friends he could get. Sierra deserved something good in her life, and if Spencer made her happy then he would be happy for her. Although he had to wonder what Trey thought about them.

Sarah eased into the chair beside the sofa. "We haven't officially met. I'm Sarah."

He noticed her left hand bore no rings. "I'm John. It's nice to meet you." He flashed a smile. Although he knew her name, she was correct in saying they'd never met. He'd heard one of the other ladies calling her Sarah earlier in the kitchen. "How do you know Bailey?"

"She's more of an acquaintance. A friend of a friend." She looked around the room. "Have you noticed everyone here has coupled up?"

His eyes widened—she was right! Stephen sat in a corner with his arm around Bailey talking with Mark and

Nicole who held hands, and Spencer and Sierra still stood in the kitchen. Trey was nowhere to be seen. "Was this a set up?" Bailey wouldn't do that, would she?

She chuckled. "Surprisingly, no. But it kind of worked out that way. Nicole tells me you remodeled Spencer's house."

He nodded. "My first."

"Wow. I heard it turned out nice."

"Thanks." He'd have to thank Bailey later for thinking to invite an even number of men to women. Sarah was beautiful, nice, and saved him from sitting there alone. And bonus, she seemed interested in him. "We should get coffee sometime."

"I'd like that." She flashed perfect teeth.

His heart tripped. Yep, he definitely owed Bailey a huge thank you.

CHAPTER THIRTEEN

SPENCER'S HANDS TIGHTENED AROUND THE STEERING wheel of his pickup. He'd expected nothing less from Mrs. Drake. He felt for Sierra and her son—moving wasn't cheap. Finding a suitable place to live in three-weeks' time while working fulltime would be a challenge.

He wanted to help her but knew of no way. He had three bedrooms at his place, but knew she'd never go for that. Their dinner was probably off, too. He could sure do without the Mrs. Drakes of the world.

He might not be able to help Sierra with her housing problem, but he could help the Belafontes by finding whoever was targeting their company. There had to be someone they'd angered that they weren't remembering. He'd check into the Davis dude but didn't expect that to go anywhere. Since the suspect who spray-painted their clients' wall appeared to be female, the couple Rick had fired last fall sounded more promising—especially since there were no other female suspects. Then again someone could be randomly targeting them. But that made little sense.

He pulled up to his house, killed the engine, then went inside. This place felt more like home, thanks to Sierra and John, and one way or another he would help them. The perpetrator had grown more brazen. What would be next?

Monday morning Sierra sat at the computer beside Bailey looking for a new place to live. "I will never agree to long-term housesit again. That woman has no idea how much she's set me back." Both financially and personally. Although Trey played it cool, she could tell he was nervous about where they'd land next.

"I agree. She's clueless," Bailey said. "I really like that you're living in Sunriver. One of us is always either in Bend or here if we need to meet with a client. It's convenient, and Sunriver is so much closer to La Pine. It's really a nice central location."

"Yes. That's an advantage, but I don't see how I can afford to live here full time."

"I looked online this morning hoping to help you find a place, but the rental market is high. Seems to make more sense to buy if you can."

"Maybe." After living these past weeks in a house, she had no desire to move back into an apartment. It was so nice not hearing her neighbors through the walls or be awakened at all hours of the night by someone vacuuming or playing loud music. "I suppose I have enough saved for a down payment on a small house, but I'd planned to put it toward Trey's college fund."

"Didn't you tell me he has a four point GPA?"

Sierra nodded. "I know what you're thinking, but there's more to getting scholarships than good grades. He needs to score high on the ACT or SAT."

"Then get him in a prep course that will prepare him.

As smart as Trey is, his college education shouldn't cost you a house."

"You might be right. But there's no way I will find a house in three weeks and have escrow close that fast."

"Maybe you could stay here for a week or two. The place is certainly big enough."

"True." But did she really want to live at work. *No way!* "There has to be another option."

"I'm not seeing it if there is." Bailey closed out the screen. "Have you heard from Spencer?"

"No. Why would I?"

"The two of you seemed cozy last night."

"I have no idea what you're talking about. Just because we were talking doesn't mean we were cozy. Spencer is a good friend, but that's the end of it." Did it have to be? Trey was warming up to him, and he was such a great guy. If she were honest, she wished his house wasn't finished because she enjoyed dropping in on him to check the progress. She'd noticed a vulnerability in him lately that she appreciated—as though he was softer somehow and not the tough cop all the time.

"Oh." She frowned. "I was hoping."

"Why?" From what she knew of Bailey, she wasn't a busybody, so her interest in Sierra's love life was weird.

"Spencer helped me out a few months ago, and I have a soft spot for him." She shrugged. "I want to see him happy, and I think you make him happy." She quickly added. "Not that he's said anything, but I can tell he's lonely, and he seems to really like you. And don't forget, he asked you to help him with the mentor program. If he didn't like you, he wouldn't have."

Sierra's head jerked back slightly. "How'd you know

he asked me to help with that?" And was her boss right? Did Spencer request her help because he had feelings for her, or at the least because he was interested?

"Nicole told me."

"Oh." It made sense that she'd know since Mark and Spencer worked closely together.

"Knock. Knock." John ambled into the room. "Good morning, ladies."

Sierra grinned. "You're in a good mood this morning. Did they find the—"

"No." He eased onto the loveseat against the wall beside the door. "I'm here for an entirely different reason." His face glowed. "Bailey, do you remember doing a proposal for a hotel in Bend?"

"Of course. But they said they were going a different direction."

"As it turned out, the new direction was selling the place. They are under new ownership, and they saw and liked your proposal. The job is ours."

A little squeal escaped Sierra's lips. "That's the best news I've heard in days! When do we start?" As much as her housing crisis needed to be addressed, she welcomed the distraction of a big project.

He filled them in on the details. "I don't have to tell you how big this is. They liked your original proposal, Bailey, but would also like for you to submit one more for their two executive suites."

Bailey frowned. "Why did they go through you and not contact me?"

She had a point. Bailey ran Belafonte Designs, not John.

"The new owner is a friend," John said.

"Did you tell them about the vandal?" Sierra asked. It didn't seem right taking on a job that might endanger the hotel guests.

"No. It's irrelevant."

"I disagree. What if someone happens upon our vandal in the act and gets assaulted? It's much more likely at a hotel."

"Or not," John said. "They have an excellent surveillance system. The vandal won't risk being discovered. I predict she will continue to go after our unoccupied homes."

Bailey frowned. "Except she didn't."

John sighed. "You're right, but I still believe this will be fine. And if you ladies will pitch in and do some manual labor there's a bonus in it for you."

Sierra wrinkled her nose. "What kind of manual labor? I don't like saws or nail guns. They scare me."

He chuckled. "Painting mostly."

She looked to Bailey who seemed to be considering the idea.

"That would be a huge undertaking considering we have other clients." Bailey looked ready to say no to painting. "What happened to the usual crew?"

"They'll be there. But the hotel is on a tight timeline, and we need to move fast." John focused his attention on Sierra. "Would Trey be willing to help? We would pay him minimum wage."

"I'm sure he'd jump at the opportunity, especially with summer approaching, but I'll have to ask to know for sure."

"Of course. Let me know ASAP."

"Sure thing."

"All right then. I'm out."

"You're not going up to see your mom?" Bailey asked.

"I did before I came in here. I have an appointment with Sarah. I'm buying a piece of property to build on."

"Congratulations!" Sierra couldn't be more pleased for him. Maybe she should check into the local housing market more seriously. She loved her job, especially now that she was being allowed to design. Although Trey had not been happy about moving here in the beginning, he'd adjusted well and had discovered many things that Sunriver had to offer. He would be bummed if he wouldn't be around for the summer season. The swimming pools had been a huge positive to his way of thinking.

The idea of randomly choosing a real estate agent didn't appeal. Spencer could probably recommend someone. She'd be sure to give him a call later.

"What do you think?" Bailey asked.

"About what?"

"Didn't you hear anything I said?" Dismay filled her voice.

"No. Sorry. My mind was a million miles away. John got me to thinking that buying a house might be the way to go. But I'm all yours now. What do you need?"

"I need you to take the rest of the day off and figure out your housing situation, and then I need you to come back tomorrow ready to work."

Sierra ducked her chin. That was as close to a reprimand as she'd ever received from Bailey, but she really shouldn't be here if she wasn't going to focus. "Umm. Do you think you could manage without me this week?"

"You want the entire week off?" Bailey's brow raised. "Are you sure you need that much time?"

"I don't *want* to take the week off, but Mrs. Drake put me in a bind, and until I figure out a couple of things, I think I'll be useless here. I need to meet with a bank about getting pre-approved for a loan. And I want to have my head one-hundred percent focused when I'm working." When she'd made up her mind to try and buy a place she didn't know, but it seemed like the best course to follow.

"Whatever you need, Sierra." Bailey stood and walked around her desk. "But we have that hotel job in Bend which will need your full attention no later than Monday."

"Understood. And I'll let John know about painting later today." Excitement bubbled. She was going to do this—ack, she was *really* going to buy a house—the only thing that terrified her more was being pregnant at sixteen and then finding herself on her own a year after Trey was born.

Her choices hadn't always been the best or easy, but this felt right. She gathered her stuff and stood. "Thanks, Bailey."

"Sure. I hope everything goes smoothly."

CHAPTER FOURTEEN

JOHN SPOTTED SIERRA SITTING ON A bench in the village with slumped shoulders. What was that all about and why was she here? Shouldn't she be working? He strolled over to her. "Mind if I join you?"

She jumped slightly and looked up. "Hi. I didn't see you. Of course." She moved over.

"Everything okay?" Had something else happened at one of the Belafonte sites that he hadn't yet heard about?

"I'm fine."

He hadn't asked how she was in so many words, but clearly she wasn't fine as she claimed, and it wasn't work related—at least it didn't appear to be. "Does this have something to do with your son's dad?"

She shook her head. "Please. I can't deal with thinking about him today, too."

So he was right. Something was up. "I know you said you're fine, but I'd like to help if I can."

"There's nothing you can do." She glanced his way. Hopelessness filled her eyes.

His gut tightened. Whatever was troubling her appeared to be big. "I hope this doesn't sound too forward, but it's clear to me that something is wrong. I'd like to help, but if you don't want it, I understand. That being said, don't forget to pray. I'm not an in-your-face religious kind of person, but the Lord is always there, and I know

He will help you deal with whatever is distressing you."

A tiny smile lifted her lips. "Thanks for the reminder. I should have done that first before leaping into buying a house."

"Not the experience you expected?"

"Not even close. I don't know what I'm going to do, but I am going to pray like you suggested."

"Good. It looks like my work here is done." He stood. "Do you have someplace to be?"

"I do. My meeting with Sarah went well earlier, and I asked her out for coffee."

A smile lit Sierra's eyes. "I don't know her well, but she seems nice. I'm glad the dinner wasn't a complete waste."

Why would she think her party had been a waste? What an odd thing to say. "On the contrary. Let me know how things go." He set out toward Brewed Awakenings and couldn't help wondering why Sierra wasn't working. Shouldn't she have heaps of work now that they had the hotel contract? Odd. But he did not oversee Sierra. That was Bailey's job, and he wouldn't interfere.

He spotted Sarah at a distance and waved to get her attention. She looked professional in a black straight skirt and blazer, with impossibly high heels. She waved back. A smile lit her face. How had he never met her before? He ambled up to her. "Hey, there."

She grinned. "Thanks for not standing me up."

"That's been a problem in the past?" He opened the door allowing her to enter first.

"You have no idea." She rolled her eyes. "One would think scheduling an appointment, or a coffee date in this case would mean something, but some people apparently don't look at their calendars."

"I see." He couldn't imagine anyone standing up the lovely woman by his side. He paid for the coffees, waited for them, then they found an out-of-the way table.

"Any progress on the vandalism?"

"Not that I've heard." He really didn't want to talk about work issues, especially in public where anyone could overhear. "So tell me what you do for fun?"

Her eyes widened a bit, but she recovered quickly at his sudden change in topic. "I'm a bit of a tennis fanatic. You'll find me on the court whenever the weather permits. How about you?"

So that was where her trim, athletic physique came from. "I enjoy running."

"You grew up around here, right?" She sipped her caramel macchiato.

He nodded.

"You don't play golf? With all the courses I'd think it would be a given."

"From time to time, but it's not a passion." He was still figuring that out. He'd thoroughly enjoyed working on Spencer's house. It broke up the monotony of going to the office day in and day out. It had been difficult juggling the remodel with running the business. "Before my dad died I enjoyed hiking."

"Why'd that change?" She propped an elbow onto the table and rested her chin on her palm.

"My brothers and I had to take over and fill in the hole Dad left. I suddenly found myself overwhelmed with work. I guess I got out of the habit of having fun then forgot how. I'm trying to change that." He grinned. Having coffee with Sarah was one step in the right direction.

She nodded. "It sounds funny, but I can see how that could happen to someone. Nicole, you remember her, right?"

He nodded. She was married to Mark, the cop working on their case.

"Well, when she first came to Sunriver she expressed a similar sentiment. I don't know why it's easy for me to keep my friends and hobbies intact where others sometimes lose themselves in their work, but we're all different. Maybe I'm a little more self-absorbed." Her eyes widened. "I probably shouldn't have admitted that on a first date."

He chuckled. "I like your honesty." Sarah's animated expressions captivated him. She knew how to put a person at ease and make him feel like the only person in the room.

"We should play tennis together sometime."

He shook his head. "I'd be no match for you. I'm a casual player at best. You could run with me sometime."

"Or not. Running is boring."

He held his fist to his chest. "You wound me. Running is not boring."

She laughed. "Compared to tennis it is."

He shrugged. "To each his own." They might not have any sports hobbies in common, but it didn't matter. This woman intrigued him, and he looked forward to getting to know her.

Spencer rested his elbows on his dining room table and

rubbed the back of his neck. It had been a long day, but not without a couple of victories. He couldn't wait to tell Sierra, but if he called her, he'd also have to admit they were no closer to figuring out who had been vandalizing the Belafonte projects. He didn't want to disappoint her, but maybe he could soften the bad news with his other news.

He palmed his phone and pressed her number in his contacts.

"Hello?" She sounded tired.

"It's Spencer. You okay?"

"Yeah. What's up?"

Something in her tone said otherwise. "You at home?"

"Yes. Why?"

"I'm on my way over." He grabbed his keys and headed out the door.

"I'm tired, Spencer."

"So am I, and I haven't eaten yet. How does Chinese sound?"

"Wonderful. I still need to make dinner. But I promised *you* dinner, not the other way around."

"Next time. I'll see you soon."

Thirty minutes later, he stood at Sierra's front door and rang the bell. She pulled the door open and relief poured over him. She looked tired, but otherwise fine. He held up two white bags. "I have sweet and sour chicken, fried rice, wontons, and a couple of other things the sales person recommended. I wasn't sure what you and Trey like."

She led the way to the dining room table. "We like everything." She swiveled and called down the hall. "Trey. Food's here."

The kid bolted from his room and slowed as soon as he spotted Spencer. "Hey." Although he didn't smile, the look of hate he'd once displayed toward Spencer was gone.

Relief washed over Spencer. "I hope you're hungry. I brought enough to feed a crowd."

"You'll need it with my son's appetite."

"I'm sitting right here," Trey said drily.

Spencer chuckled. "Dig in."

"After we pray," Sierra said. She offered a short blessing over the food, and when she opened her eyes they locked on his.

His insides jolted. She had an effect on him that he hadn't expected. Or was it the prayer, which included thanking God for him—that was a first.

"Did you get fortune cookies?" Trey asked.

Spencer pulled his gaze from Sierra and focused on Trey. "Sure did. That small bag has them."

"My son likes to indulge in dessert before the main course." Her eyes twinkled. "But he knows better, right?" She looked to Trey.

"Yes, ma'am." His eyes looked down.

They filled their plates with way too much food and dug in with fancy chopsticks Sierra had found in a drawer. "I actually came over tonight to tell you something."

"Oh?" Sierra raised a brow.

"I know this isn't ideal, but it will buy you a little time. A buddy of mine is going on a short-term mission trip. He'll be out of the country for a month and leaves in two weeks. I told him about your situation, and he said you and Trey could use his place while he's gone. I know you have three weeks left here, but it will provide time to find a more permanent place." He couldn't read Sierra's face. He thought she'd be happy, but she looked more perplexed—or maybe it was surprised.

"I don't know what to say except I've spent the day praying about our housing situation. I didn't realize that escrow would take at least thirty days and had given up buying a house because of that—we would be homeless before we could get into a house." She shook her head and wonder shone in her eyes. "Shortly before you called about dinner I felt peace about our situation. I didn't expect the answer would be housesitting someone else's home."

"The Lord works in mysterious ways," he said.

She raised a brow.

"What? Just because I didn't grow up in church doesn't mean I haven't heard that phrase, and honestly, I think He does work in mysterious ways."

"I thought you weren't a Christian." Trey eyed him then took a bite of orange chicken.

"About that—my status has changed. That prophecy stuff is rather compelling. It's hard for me to deny that God exists. I've seen too much to prove otherwise." His gaze snagged Sierra's—her eyes glistened.

"I had no idea you'd made a decision to become a Christian. Why didn't you say anything?"

He shrugged. "I just did."

"Tell us more. When did it happen?" Sierra looked ready to burst.

He had no idea his decision would be such a big deal to her, then again maybe he should have known based on Mark's nudging him to go to church. The book of John outlined pretty well how he should pray. "You knew I was interested in Bible prophecy. I dug into the verses the speaker had used and then started reading the Bible from the beginning of the New Testament. I've read a *lot* since that night. To be honest, it was difficult to put it down."

"You understood it?"

"Not everything. But I attended church some when I was younger, so it wasn't completely foreign to me. I also picked Mark's brain a little and met with the pastor at your church." He'd planned to ask her a few questions, but his meeting with the pastor cleared up a lot.

"I'm very happy for you." Sierra grinned. "I'm glad you have Mark, too. He seemed like a good guy when he was here the other night."

"He is. That's another thing I wanted to talk with you about." He noticed that Trey was still devouring food but listening intently to their conversation. He hadn't planned to bring this up in front of the teen, but why not? He had nothing to lose. "The mentor program was given the go ahead on a trial basis."

"What's that?" Trey asked. He stopped eating and looked directly at him.

"Teens or even kids can sign up at the police station to have a mentor."

"What does that mean?"

"For example, if I was your mentor we'd hang out together doing things you enjoy."

"Oh."

Anticipation filled him. "I was hoping I could be your mentor."

Trey's head jerked. "Why? I don't need a mentor."

"I thought it'd be fun, but if you're not interested no one will force you to participate. The idea is to have a blast doing things together. I was thinking how close summer break is. You'll be stuck at home alone while your mom is working, without the distraction of school. I happen to have Thursday and Friday off, so I'm free to hang out with my mentee. We could do whatever you'd like."

"Really?" Doubt filled the teen's eyes.

"Sure. Anything."

Trey's face brightened. "I suppose we could give it a shot. Do you fish?"

"I do. And I have a canoe."

Trey shrugged, but a grin tugged at his mouth. "It's not like forever. You said it's a trial?"

Spencer nodded. "That's right."

"I'd like to try fishing."

"Then that's the first thing we'll do when the season opens. In the meantime we could go canoeing." Things were working out much better than he'd expected.

"Any progress on the vandalism?" Sierra asked.

He blew out a breath, long and slow. "Not yet. Honestly, we have a higher priority case, and since no one appears to be in any danger from this vandal . . . I'm sorry." Hopefully things would slow down and they would have time to follow up on the leads. "If someone was in imminent danger it'd be different."

"I understand. You need to work on the most pressing things first. But that won't stop me from doing my own investigating."

Trey's eyes widened, and he shook his head. "No way, Mom."

"Why not? Someone needs to stop this woman. All I have to do is figure out who she is."

Spencer admired her tenacity, but she could get hurt.

"I have to agree with your son. You should leave this to the police."

She crossed her arms. "Police who are too busy to do anything about the vandalism. Don't worry, I won't put myself in a dangerous situation."

"The funny thing about that is, we often don't recognize danger until it's too late. So far nothing has happened, but if you provoke this person . . ." Spencer let his words sink in. Let her take what she wanted from them—he only hoped she wouldn't put herself in harm's way over a few pranks.

"I'm a smart woman. I think I can handle it." Determination shone in her eyes.

He sighed. "Fine, but let me know what you're up to. If I can, I want to be there with you."

"Me, too." Trey's brow furrowed. He wiped his mouth on a napkin. "May I be excused?"

Sierra nodded.

"Thanks for dinner, Spencer," Trey said.

"Sure." Now to convince Sierra to wait for the police. No way did he want her getting hurt because he was too busy working another case.

CHAPTER FIFTEEN

Sierra stood outside High Desert Interior Design in the Sunriver business loop. She'd never noticed the place before, but it had to be where Celia worked. She pushed inside and paused. The place reminded her of something, but she couldn't quite place what.

"Good morning, may I help you?" A woman she presumed was Celia approached her.

"Not really. I was curious about your store, so I decided to check it out."

Celia smiled, but it didn't reach her eyes. "Feel free to look around. I do a lot of antiquing, and the owner has sent many things from her travels abroad."

"Thank you." Sierra walked around and noted the prices were marked up pretty high. She wouldn't be purchasing anything here for her clients. She glanced toward the cash register where Celia watched her every move with anger-filled eyes.

Irritation flowed through Sierra. What did she ever do to this woman? Maybe she should buy something regardless of the high prices—it would be worth it to get that look out of Celia's eyes. She shivered.

A flash of memory hit her—Celia had been in one of her design classes. She'd caught the attention of their instructor and had been the teacher's pet. How could she have forgotten?

Sierra fingered an antique wall sconce. It was designed for candles, but it wouldn't take much work to wire it for a bulb. The price was surprisingly reasonable compared to many of the other items on display. She turned and caught her breath. The woman stood inches from her—talk about invading her space. "What are you doing?" She stepped aside allowing more room between them and crossed her arms. This was ridiculous.

"Nothing. You like the sconce?"

"It has promise." She looked to the sconce then back at the woman. They say kindness is the better route to take and as difficult as it was to be nice to Celia, she would do her best. "I'll take it."

"Great." Celia took it to the register and wrapped it first in paper then bubble wrap. "This is a nice piece. I wondered why Mr. Belafonte chose you over me, considering I graduated top in our class and you lack experience for someone of your age."

She ignored the jab at her age—talk about ageism. "You remember me?"

"Of course. You were the oldest in our class. It was hard not to notice you."

Okay, ignoring her rudeness was becoming more difficult.

"As I was saying. I can see why you were chosen over me. You have excellent taste."

"And tact too. Something someone with your *youth* clearly lacks." She handed over a twenty-dollar bill. She never should have come in here.

Celia's face hardened. "Touché." She placed the sconce in a fancy paper shopping bag and gave it to Sierra. "Have a nice day."

"Thank you. I will." She walked to the door then turned. "Out of curiosity, who owns this place?"

"My godmother."

She chuckled. "As in your fairy godmother. Cute, but seriously. Who owns this place?"

Celia raised a brow and crossed her arms. "Clarissa Drake. I believe you are staying in her house."

Dread whooshed over Sierra, and she stepped back. "Oh. I thought you were messing around and making a joke about your fairy godmother—I mean godmother, since you seem to like working here so much." She offered a smile that was greeted by a hard stare. "Never mind." She left the shop, wishing she'd never entered. Clearly Celia had issues, but why did she seem to dislike Sierra so much? Because she got the job and Celia hadn't?

Sierra spotted her Realtor, Patience, beside her car in the parking lot and waved. She ambled over to her. "I hope you weren't waiting long."

"I just got here. Did you find a treasure?"

"Perhaps. Time will tell." She looked over her shoulder and saw Celia watching from the window. An uneasy feeling crept over her. Could Celia be behind the vandalism? She shoved the thought away. The girl wasn't the nicest, but that didn't make her a vandal.

Sierra kicked off her shoes as she entered Mrs. Drake's house. This place no longer felt like home, and the sooner they moved the better. "I'm here." She strolled into the guest room—no Trey. *Odd.* "Trey!" She called out as she wandered through the house. No response.

Panic bubbled as her pace picked up. She flung open one door after another in search of her son. Where was he? He knew better than to leave the house without telling her. She checked her phone—maybe she'd missed a text. "Where are you?" She asked as she typed the message into her phone. She tapped her toe, waiting for a reply.

Why wasn't he responding? Her phone finally chimed.

Canoeing.

She let out her breath in a whoosh. "Next time let me know ahead of time. I freaked out when you weren't here." She had a habit of talking as she typed her texts. She ought to use the speech to text mode and save a little effort, but never thought about it until after the fact.

He had to be with Spencer since they'd talked about canoeing over dinner last night—but shouldn't he have at least told her what they were up to? Somehow the man had wiggled into their lives without her realizing it was happening. The odd thing was, she didn't mind. Even if Trey neglected to communicate that he was out with Spencer. He was a good man, and if he could be a positive role model for her son, then all the better.

At least Trey no longer brought up the desire to meet his dad—one less thing for her to worry about. Not that worrying did an ounce of good. No, all worry did was add stress lines to her face.

A text chimed in from Trey. She read it. Spencer wanted to come over for dinner again. Her stomach fluttered quickly followed by unease. Her feelings for this man were moving like a speeding freight train. She wasn't looking for a relationship, but yet everywhere she turned

Spencer was there.

Somehow she'd thought if any man was going to grab her heart, it would be John. He was gorgeous, rich, independent, a strong Christian, and they had similar interests, but there was no spark between them. He was a great friend—no more, no less. But Spencer made her feel something again. He was a rock—strong, intelligent, handsome, caring, and had a huge heart. The fact that he cared enough about her son to reach out to him put him in a category of his own.

Could there ever be something between them, or was she only attracted to him because he'd been there for her and her son? Whatever the case, she didn't have time to ponder it right now. She had dinner to prepare and a phone call to make. She called Bailey. "Hey, there."

"How's the house hunt going?"

"Great. I found a sweet little house on the south side near the village, and Spencer hooked us up with someone who will be out of town for a month. We can stay at his place while we wait for escrow to close."

"That's fantastic news. So does that mean I can expect you back at work tomorrow?"

Guilt washed over her. "Absolutely." Other than trying to figure out who was out to get the Belafonte business interests, she'd given little to no thought about the new project they were starting on Monday, and it would be a lot of work even if the current owner approved all their original ideas.

"I'm actually calling because I found that new interior design place today."

"Really?" Interest piqued Bailey's voice. "And?"

"It has a storefront with several nice pieces, but that's

not why I'm calling. The woman working there is none other than Celia."

"Do I know this woman?"

"Yes. She's the other person who interviewed for my job. We were talking about her at the party I hosted."

"That's right. So what has you so excited about the place?"

"The owner is Mrs. Drake."

"You're kidding!"

"Nope. When she told me she had business interests in town I never imagined she was in competition with us. What I don't get is why she hired us to do her place."

"That's odd." Her voice had turned reflective.

"I don't know why, but I sensed a weird vibe from Celia."

"Explain what you mean."

"She made it very clear she doesn't like me for starters. Yet I've never done anything to her. We had some classes together, and *she* was the teacher's pet. Not me. She seemed jealous of me getting this job, but at the same time, she stated she loved what she was doing. Apparently Mrs. Drake is her godmother."

"The plot thickens," Bailey said. "This is all so strange. I'm glad you're moving out of her place. She's always made me feel uneasy, but now even more so."

"I can understand why." Sierra prided herself on being a good judge of character, but she'd missed the mark with Mrs. Drake.

"Any news from Spencer about the vandalism?"

"Nothing other than we are a low priority."

Bailey sighed. "I was afraid of that."

"Don't worry. I'm working on it, too. It frosts me that

someone is targeting Belafonte Design and the construction branch of the business. This is an environmentally conscious company, and we treat people right. There's no good reason to be targeting us."

"I agree. You don't think Mrs. Drake could be behind this do you?"

"She's not a nice woman, but no. If Mrs. Drake was out to hurt our business, I'm sure she'd come up with a much more ingenious method. I mean really, vandalism. She could do far worse than that if she wanted to hurt us."

"Good point. The more I think about it, the more I feel like it's a disgruntled former employee or bored kids."

"I suppose you're right. Well, I should go. Spencer's coming over for dinner, and I need to figure out what to serve."

"Are you seeing each other?" Bailey gasped. "I'm sorry. That's none of my business. I shouldn't have asked."

"It's fine. We're not officially seeing each other. He's doing a mentor thing and Trey is his mentee. I offered to make him dinner a while back, and he's collecting."

"I see. So you'll be at work tomorrow?"

"I'll be there. 'Bye." She disconnected the call wondering at the tone in Bailey's voice. What did she mean by *I see*? She'd almost sounded like she was skeptical of her relationship with Spencer, but she was too professional to call her on it. Whatever, there was too much to do to stand around thinking about what her boss thought about her personal life. She had a knock-your-socks-off dinner to prepare.

Three hours later, Sierra had the table set for three, a roasted chicken resting on the cutting board, and a coconut curry soup with quinoa ready to dish up. The front door opened and the guys sauntered in.

"Hey, Mom." Trey stood in the entryway, his mouth pulled into a wide grin.

She took in his contented look and the smile that lit Spencer's eyes. "I take it you enjoyed yourselves."

"We did," Trey said. He sniffed the air. "What's for dinner? It smells good.""

"Coconut curry soup and chicken."

He wrinkled his nose. "Hmm. That's new."

Panic hit her. Why had she tried out a new recipe on a guest? She forced a smile. "Well, it sounded good when I spotted the recipe on Pinterest, so we'll see. The two of you get to be my guinea pigs. Go wash up. Dinner's ready."

"Lead the way," Spencer said.

She had to hand it to the man. Her son seemed happier than she'd seen him since Christmas morning, and Spencer looked pretty good himself. He wore the outdoorsman ensemble well. From his jeans to the flannel shirt, he appeared comfortable and content.

When was the last time she'd truly felt content? She couldn't remember.

"I'm starved!" Trey said as he approached the table.

She quickly dished up their soup, added the bowls to the table, then placed the platter with the chicken in the center.

Spencer looked at the spread with appreciation in his eyes. "If this tastes half as good as it smells, you found a winner."

Warmth filled her. How did one man's praise make her feel content from head to toe? She tucked the thought away and instead flashed a smile. "I hope so."

The meal went off without a hitch and the guys loved

the new recipe. She'd set that one aside as a keeper. Trey excused himself and Sierra watched as her son wandered off to his room grinning. Maybe Trey really did need a man in his life to do the kind of things with him he'd missed out on doing with his dad. "It looks like you had quite a day. I haven't seen my son so content and happy in a long time. What happened?"

"I'm not really sure." Spencer shrugged. "But I'm not complaining. It's such a relief to have him look at me with something other than hate or anger. You have a good son."

"Thanks. It's not always been easy, but with the Lord's help I've done my best."

He chuckled. "I'm going to have to get used to the way Christians talk."

"It's more than talk—at least for me."

"I can see that." He looked around the room and motioned toward the kitchen. "Would you like help with the dishes?"

"Now there's an offer I can't refuse." Spencer's charm seemed to have not only worked on her son, but her as well, because right now she wanted to nullify her pledge to remain single.

CHAPTER SIXTEEN

MONDAY MORNING, JOHN SAT BEHIND HIS desk in the Bend office, once again wishing to be anywhere other than there. Work at the hotel here in town began today, and it would be all hands on deck once the plan was approved—he only awaited word from Bailey.

The door opened and Sarah walked in.

A tingle zipped through him. He stood. "This is a surprise! What brings you by?"

"You mentioned your boredom with office work, so since I was in Bend, I thought I'd stop in to say hi."

"I'm glad you did. Have a seat." He motioned to the chair situated in front of his desk.

"Thanks. But there's another reason I stopped in. I got to thinking about your vandalism situation."

He raised a brow. "And?"

"Well, here's the thing. I had some friends who got into trouble with the law last summer. They seem to be in the know when it comes to illegal activities in this area. I could ask them if they've heard anything if you'd like me to."

He almost recoiled. How could such a kind woman have friends like that? Maybe dating Sarah wasn't such a good idea after all. No, he was being judgmental. She had to have a good reason for staying friends with them.

"I might be volunteering prematurely. I haven't

spoken to them since they used me to break into houses."

"They did what?" Now he *had* to know what happened.

"It's a long story, but I used to moonlight at a property management company to help pay off my debt. My friends came to work with me when they were visiting, and while I wasn't paying attention, they accessed the company computers to find out which homes were unoccupied. They, along with a couple of guys, would break in and steal electronic equipment and anything else they thought was of value."

"Right. I remember reading about that in the paper. But I had no idea you were involved."

"Only as their unsuspecting patsy." She shook her head. "I'm still reeling over what they did, but I'm willing to ask them about the vandalism."

"No. I don't want to put you in that kind of position. The police will handle it."

"That's just it. I heard from Nicole and Bailey that the police had more pressing things to deal with."

He ran a hand along the back of his neck. "True, but things have been quiet the past few days—not one problem at any of our work sites has been reported. Maybe they've found something else to occupy their time."

"That's doubtful. Those crimes were directed at Belafonte job sites for a reason, and people like that don't stop until they get what they want."

"What do you think they want?" He'd love to hear an outsider's opinion. His brothers were convinced it was the job of a disgruntled past employee.

"Beats me."

He sighed. "Yeah. Me too." They had to be missing

something or someone. The only two employees any of them could come up with accounted for their whereabouts during the time the vandalism was suspected to have happened. What were they missing? His phone rang. He checked the number—blocked. "Belafonte Construction. John speaking."

Silence.

"Hello?"

Nothing.

He disconnected the call as unease gripped him.

Spencer sat in a closed-door meeting with Mark and the Belafonte brothers. Each of them had received phone calls with silence on the other end. Ordinarily he would think little of it, but considering everything that had happened, he and Mark decided to bring the brothers into the PD.

Mark flipped a pen back and forth between his fingers. "So all of the calls came from blocked numbers, and you couldn't hear anything at all in the background?"

The men all nodded.

Spencer frowned. It would be more helpful if they'd heard typing, a train, voices in the distance, a horn honking—anything that would give them something to work with, but complete silence didn't move their investigation forward. "I'm afraid there's nothing we can do with that. I suggest installing surveillance cameras around your construction sites, and as far as design jobs go, don't tell anyone where you are working, and ask your clients and workers to stay quiet."

Stephen shook his head. "How are we supposed to do that without scaring them away? And forget about keeping the contractors quiet. There's no way we can enforce that."

John sat up straighter. "What if we do a promotion of sorts? We take before and after photos and then put it on our website for people to vote on. The winner will get fifty percent off the cost of labor. But the homeowners must sign a confidentiality agreement to be eligible. I know it doesn't address the problem of all the workers, but it would help, and it might even be good for business."

"I like it," Stephen said. "Will you work on that, John? In the meantime we'll get security cameras set up at the site where Rick is currently building."

Spencer liked how the men thought, but it didn't change anything. They were no closer to knowing who was targeting the Belafontes. "Meanwhile, Mark and I will work on following any leads that come up."

Rick stood. "Okay, then. If we're done here, I have work to do."

Spencer nodded. "We'll be in touch."

The brothers filed out the door.

Spencer looked to Mark. "What do you think?"

The other man blew out a long breath. "Either they angered the wrong person, or we have a series of coincidences."

"I don't believe in coincidence—at least not that many."

Mark frowned. "Me either. Too bad we were unable to pull any usable evidence from the areas that were vandalized. It turned out the spray paint was already on site, so we couldn't even track its purchase."

"That in itself is a clue." Spencer leaned forward. "They didn't bring the paint, so either they hadn't intended to leave a message, but they did it anyway, or they knew there'd be spray paint onsite, and it was all part of the bigger plan. They wanted the Belafontes to know they were being targeted and that the vandalism wasn't random."

Mark's brow rose. "I suppose they could have brought their own method of displaying their message but when they saw the spray can used that instead."

"It's possible. At this point, we need to wait and see if they strike again in front of the surveillance cameras."

"Agreed." Spencer stood. "I'll step up patrols near the houses they are working on here in Sunriver, but their Bend projects are out of our jurisdiction."

Too bad the hotel job was in Bend. If Spencer were a betting man, he'd say that would be their most logical target. It was no secret that they'd won the contract, and if they kept their other jobs quiet, the hotel was a no-brainer. He'd alert the Bend police to what was going on, but first he'd give Bailey and Sierra a heads up.

CHAPTER SEVENTEEN

SIERRA STROLLED THROUGH THE HOTEL THEY would be redecorating. The place was in dire need of an update. Worn green carpet lined the hall leading to the bank of rooms where they would begin. Fortunately, replacing the carpet in the entire hotel was on the to-do list.

Sierra would tape off and paint one room at a time then the carpet installers would do their magic. The rest would be easy by comparison. At least she wasn't responsible for painting every room. John and Bailey promised professional painters would be hired, too.

She stopped in the gift shop and bought a pack of M&M's and a bottle of water then turned and nearly ran into a woman. "Excuse me." *Celia?*

"Fancy meeting you here," Celia said. A stiff smile lifted her lips.

"I was thinking the same thing. Are you a guest?" What a dumb question. Obviously she wasn't since she lived in the area. Besides, they only had one wing of the hotel open right now due to the work being done.

"No. A friend is in town."

Sierra nodded. "Have fun with your friend."

"I will." Celia sidestepped Sierra and rushed toward the registration desk.

Odd. She strolled down the hall toward the room she would be working in and stopped in the open doorway.

John stood at the window looking out onto the parking lot. "Is everything okay?"

He turned. "I think so. Why do you ask?"

She shrugged. "I didn't expect to see you here." Spencer had called her yesterday warning her to be aware of her surroundings at all times while working at the hotel. He'd kind of freaked her out, but at the same time, he was probably only being cautious, considering all that had been going on at their jobsites. It was what he'd said to her later that evening that had kept her awake for half the night.

Spencer had asked her out and she'd accepted. She still couldn't believe she'd said yes. They were going on a hike together this weekend. How would Trey react when he found out? Although he and Spencer seemed to have put the past behind them, she'd never dated anyone but Trey's dad.

"Are you with me, Sierra?" John asked.

"Yes, sorry. My mind wandered. Will you repeat what you said?"

He grinned. "You had an odd look on your face. If I didn't know better, I'd say you were thinking about a man."

"Ha! Why would I be doing that?"

He shrugged. "There's no crime in daydreaming about Spencer."

She gasped. "How'd you know?"

"I have eyes. Anyone paying attention can see the chemistry the two of you have."

She sucked in her bottom lip. Did that mean Trey already knew too?

"What are you worried about?"

"Trey."

He nodded. "Don't stress your son's reaction. He and I have met to jog regularly and—"

"You never said anything."

"I didn't realize I needed to. You asked me to talk with him, and I did. He reached out to me."

"I had no idea. Are you the reason he's okay with Spencer now?"

"It's possible I had a little to do with it, but your son has a mind of his own."

"That's the truth!"

He chuckled. He motioned toward the M&Ms in her hand. "I picked you up a bag too."

She placed the candy inside her purse. She hated that he was so observant. M&Ms were a vice she'd never been able to kick.

"Think fast." He flicked a bag of M&Ms at her.

She snatched it from the air. "Thanks."

He laughed.

"What?"

"Trey told me to do that. He said you never miss. I didn't believe him." He shrugged. "Looks like he may have been right."

"It's a gift. So he's the one who told you about my M&M addiction."

John only grinned. "I've alerted the hotel manager to be vigilant about security. Please keep your eyes open while you're here. Watch for anyone acting suspiciously and report it to me immediately."

Alarm bells went off inside her. "Is there something else I should know? Spencer warned me as well." She'd been freaked out when Spencer alerted her to be aware of her surroundings and anything suspicious, but then calmed since he was a cop and probably was overly cautious because of all the stuff he'd seen. John, however, was a different story.

He glanced toward the open door. "Take a walk with me."

She nodded and tore the top off her bag of candy. She poured several into her palm then tossed them into her mouth. She bit through the candy coating and let the chocolate melt in her mouth. *Mmm.* She strode beside John until they got to the parking lot. He moved to an area with nothing around where no one would be able to lurk unnoticed.

"We received a threat," John said.

Sierra's pulse kicked into double time. "Tell me about it."

"It was in a note taped to the door at my mom's house warning us to back off."

"What's that supposed to mean? What are we supposed to back off from?"

"We don't know. But our case is now a priority for the police."

Her thoughts flew to her son. "Is Trey in any danger?"

"I don't think so, but who knows." He rubbed the base of his neck. "I'm not in this person's head. I can't say for sure about anything."

"I understand." Worry nibbled at her mind. She needed to warn her son to be aware of his surroundings at all times and no more running alone. Although it sounded like he'd been running with John. "Why didn't Spencer say anything to me about this?"

"At first we asked that this be kept on the down low,

but the more I thought about it, the more I realized it wasn't fair to stay quiet."

"I appreciate you letting me know. I need to make a call, then get to work." Her phone rang.

John nodded. "I'll let you get to it." He strode toward the hotel entrance.

She didn't recognize the caller I.D. "Hello?"

"Sierra. This is Bailey." A group of women congregated nearby laughing and talking loudly.

Sierra covered her other ear and strained to hear Bailey over the ruckus.

"Would you run to the house and pick up something for me? I need a few samples right away."

"I'm kind of busy here. Can't you get it yourself? You're a lot closer to the house than I am."

Silence.

"Bailey?" Okay, so maybe she shouldn't have questioned her. She'd never thought her boss the kind of person to act like this, but maybe she was having a bad day. The group of women came closer. Sierra moved away, but it didn't do any good.

"I can't. I really need your help."

Sierra sighed. "Are you feeling okay? Your voice sounds funny." Or maybe it was the combination of the loud women and her phone acting up. It wouldn't be the first time voices had sounded distorted in her phone.

Bailey cleared her throat. "I'm catching a cold."

"Oh." She listened as Bailey asked her to bring the carpet samples sitting by the file cabinet in her office. Funny, she didn't recall seeing any carpet. "I'll get it to you ASAP." She disconnected the call, then shot a text to John explaining she had to run an errand for Bailey at his mom's house, then she'd be back to paint.

Traffic moved along at a nice clip, and in under forty minutes Sierra pulled up to Mona's house. She slid out of her SUV. A hint of smoke tickled her nose. Someone must have lit the fireplace.

She jogged to the door and thrust it open.

Smoke! Her pulse kicked into double time. She waved a hand in front of her face and blinked her stinging eyes.

"Help! Someone help me!"

"Mona!" The older woman stood at the top of the stairs. "Stay there. I'll be right up." Sierra ducked low and took the stairs as fast as her legs would move. Her throat burned from the smoke. She coughed as she reached the top landing. "I'm here. It's going to be okay." She coughed again.

Terror covered Mona's face. She clung to Sierra's arm.

"Easy now." She blinked as if that would clear the smoke from her burning eyes. Not for the first time in her life, she wished she were bigger and stronger. Mona would take forever walking down these stairs, and there was no way she could carry the woman who stood taller than she did.

Together they eased down one step and then the next. She reached into her pocket for her cell phone to call 911 — empty. It must be in her SUV. A large form entered through the front door. "Up here. Help!" Was that a firefighter? Visibility had diminished as they continued down one step at a time. Halfway to the bottom a man who was now clearly a firefighter swooped Mona into his arms and motioned her ahead of him.

Sierra stooped low and rushed down the stairs. She swept through the front entrance and kept going until another firefighter stopped her.

"Is anyone else inside?" he asked.

"I don't think so. Mona should have been the only one home. How did you know about the fire? I left my phone in my car and didn't have time to call 911."

"Someone else must have called. Excuse me." He strode away.

She looked around for Mona and found her at the ambulance. On shaky legs, Sierra made her way over to the matriarch of the Belafonte family. "How are you, Mrs. Belafonte?"

"Considering my house is on fire. I'm doing quite well. It's a good thing my nose still works." She coughed. "I guess the smoke detectors need new batteries."

That was right . . . she hadn't heard even one going off—odd. "I'll call your family and let them know what happened." She hustled to her SUV and phoned John, then Bailey.

"Bailey, there was a fire at Mona's. It's a good thing you sent me here, or I don't think she would have made it out before she was overcome with smoke."

"There's a fire? And what do you mean I sent you there? We haven't spoken since yesterday."

John raced to his mother's house. Why had she been alone? When one of the family members couldn't be there, they made arrangements for her nurse's assistant to be there. How had the house caught fire? He pressed the gas harder, exceeding the speed limit. He'd phoned Rick before leaving the hotel. Hopefully his brother would be able to get there faster than him. He hated the idea of his mom being without one of them.

He took the Sunriver exit and eased up on the gas. His mind raced with questions that couldn't be answered. Sierra said she'd call Bailey who was with Stephen. They were the closest, so hopefully they'd already be with his mom.

His mother's driveway finally came into sight. He slowed for the turn then eased up the driveway only making it three quarters of the way because of fire trucks and a police car blocking it. He pulled over to the side so they would be able to get out.

He killed the engine then ran toward his family and Sierra gathered near her SUV.

Stephen waved. "Take it easy, John. Everyone is okay. They took Mom to St. Charles hospital as a precaution. Rick and Gail will meet her there."

"If Mom is there, why are we here?" Relief washed over him. At least his older brother and his wife were with his mom, but why hadn't anyone let him know she was being taken there? He could have been waiting for her since the hotel wasn't far from the hospital.

"Spencer needed one of us to stay here. Since you were already on your way, and I know how fast you drive, I decided not to call."

John frowned. He had a reputation for speeding but still wished they'd called. "What's wrong with Mom? And why was she alone?"

"The medics felt like she should see a doctor to make sure she was okay."

"Given her medical history, that was a good idea,"

John said.

"That's exactly what I thought," Stephen agreed. "As to why she was alone, I have no idea. I didn't think of it until you asked."

John yanked his phone from his pocket and pulled up the number for the woman who was supposed to be with his mother.

"Hello?"

"This is John Belafonte."

"Hi! How's the outing going with Mona?"

"What outing?"

"Sierra called last night and said you would be taking her on a family outing today and that you might be a little late arriving. She said I didn't need to wait."

He shook his head. That made no sense.

"Is there a problem?" Concern edged the woman's voice.

"None other than your services are no longer required." He did his best to not raise his voice, but suddenly his family's attention had shifted to him.

"Why?"

"You left my mother alone."

"Sierra said it was okay, and your mother was fine with it, too. You know I only work nights."

He did his best to explain what happened before ending the call. He turned to Sierra. "She said you called and told her someone was taking my mom on an outing?"

"I've only seen her in passing and said goodbye as she was leaving. I never deal with the night nurse, or whatever she's called. Did she say I did?"

He nodded. He didn't know what to think. He wanted to believe Sierra, but he was torn. He ran a hand through his hair. "So why exactly do we need to be here if Mom's at the hospital and the fire is out?"

Spencer approached them and cleared his throat. "The fire looks suspicious. I thought it'd be best if everyone stuck around. This could be connected to the threat against your family."

John's gut clenched. He was sick of whoever was attacking his family. Up to now it had all been harmless, but today changed things. "I wish you'd catch this person and lock him up."

"We're trying." Spencer sounded as annoyed as he did.

A firefighter walked around from the side of the house carrying a gasoline can. He walked up to Spencer. "Looks like we found the accelerant."

John couldn't believe this was happening. Who hated his family enough to start his mom's house on fire?

CHAPTER EIGHTEEN

SPENCER READ THE REPORT FROM THE fire investigator for the second time. The stack of wood in the back of the house had been doused with gasoline and lit. The fire grew and spread to the house. Thankfully, it only damaged the backside of the house and didn't start a wild fire.

Spencer looked at Mark and stilled. "What's wrong? You have that look."

"I spotted a gasoline can in the back of Sierra's SUV that is identical to the one we found. It's an antique. They don't sell these things anymore. With a fast accelerant like that, she could have easily driven from Bend then started the fire. It would be easy to wait for a bit, then go in to play the hero."

Spencer's gut tightened. "She wouldn't do that. And having a similar gas can doesn't make her guilty. It could have been there for a number of reasons."

"I agree. But she knows where the Belafonte jobsites are, she has access to all of them, the problems began after she was hired, and—"

"And she's been working as hard as anyone else to figure out who is targeting the family. I don't believe for one minute she's guilty of anything." How dare Mark suggest Sierra was the perpetrator. He clamped down on his jaw to keep from saying something he'd regret.

"Okay," Mark said. "Let's assume you're correct, and she has nothing to do with this. Explain all the coincidences."

"I can't, but they are circumstantial. You can't prove she did any of that. She had been in Bend before the fire and had no intention of going to Mona's place. Someone claiming to be Bailey phoned her and drew her to the house."

"Now we're getting someplace."

"What? You're giving up pinning this on Sierra that easily?"

He shrugged. "I never thought she was guilty. I only wanted to get a rise out of you. You always come up with better theories when you're angry."

Spencer glared at Mark. "Think we could get a warrant for the phone record? We might be able to determine who called her. My guess is it was the arsonist. He set the fire, but didn't want to kill Mona." Kill Mona . . . *Hmm.* They might have been coming at this all wrong. "We need to dig into Mona's past. See if she has any enemies."

Mark nodded. "I agree. Although the family business appears to be the target, Mona might be who they are after or the reason the business has been inundated with trouble."

"Kind of senseless considering her health issues. From what I've been told she doesn't have much longer to live."

"True. But, revenge—or whatever this is—doesn't have to make sense." Mark reached for his phone. "I'll get right on that warrant."

Spencer couldn't sit at his desk another minute. His day had barely begun and he needed to do something. Good thing he had patrol duty. It would give him time to think as well as something to keep himself busy. He headed outside and slid into the Sunriver Police Department SUV.

The cool May morning air and blue sky promised a pretty day ahead. As someone who spent his days driving around the resort community, he appreciated the beauty of the area.

He made a left out of the parking lot. He wanted to have a look at that gasoline can for himself. Hopefully he would catch Sierra before she left for Bend. A few minutes later he pulled up beside her vehicle and got out right as she exited the front door. "Good morning."

A smile lit her face. "Hi, yourself. What brings you by so early?" Her paint-splattered jeans fit her perfectly.

"That's a nice look on you."

She laughed and posed with her hands on her hips, bending one knee. "You like it. Paint clothes are all the rage on the New York runways this season." She batted her eyelashes.

"I'm sure they are." He winked. Too bad he was on duty. He wanted nothing more than to pull her close and kiss her silly. The thought startled him, yet they'd been going that direction for a couple of weeks. "Mark said he spotted a gas can in the back end of your rig. You mind if I take a look?"

Her forehead scrunched. "I don't own a gas can, much less drive around with one in my vehicle." She strode to the back end and lifted the hatchback style door. She gasped. "How did *that* get there?" She reached for it.

He grabbed her arm. "Don't touch it. I suspect it's evidence."

"For what?"

"I believe it belongs to whoever started the fire at Mona's house."

Her face paled. "Why is it in my—?" Her fear-filled gaze locked with his. "Someone is trying to set me up. Between this and that caller claiming to be Bailey."

"You could be right. We need to talk. I think you'd better call John or Bailey and let them know you're going to be late to work today."

"Can't this wait? There is so much to be done. It's all hands on deck. I have to be there."

He wanted to help her and didn't believe for one minute she'd set that fire, but he'd be remiss in his job if he didn't question her. "I suppose it could wait."

She let out her breath in a whoosh. "Thank you." Her lips turned down.

"What?"

"I won't be able to concentrate all day if I don't get this over with. I'll call Bailey."

Sierra carefully painted the edges around the window so the pros could come in with the paint sprayer and finish off the room. She couldn't get her conversation with Spencer from her mind. It had been kind of scary to be officially questioned, but she was glad it had been Spencer doing the questioning and not some cop she didn't know.

Why would someone try and make it look like she'd set the fire? The phone call made in her name to the home care provider really disturbed her too. None of this made sense. To make matters worse, Spencer seemed very bothered when she'd left. Surely he knew she was innocent.

This nightmare had to end soon. The family couldn't take much more. Poor Mona had moved in with Rick's family. At least she was no worse for wear after the fire. But she had to be rattled by living at Rick's house. She was used to a quiet, solitary life. Not one filled with the busyness that accompanied children.

They were all on edge. No one knew what would happen next. Now Sierra seemed to be the target, and she had no idea why. Her hand slipped and the paint swiped the windowsill.

"How's it going in here?"

A little scream escaped her lips. She whirled around. "John, you scared me. Next time knock first."

He frowned. "You okay? You're wound a little tight today."

"You'd be too if evidence in an arson investigation had been found in your car."

His eyes narrowed. "What are you talking about?" The jovial look on his face hardened.

"I thought you knew."

"Obviously not."

She told him what Spencer had said.

"You're serious?"

She nodded.

He rubbed the back of his neck. A flurry of emotions played across his face then his gaze met hers with regret. "I don't know what's going on, and I don't want to believe this of you, but ever since you started working for us we've had problems. I know this isn't the right thing to do, but until you can be proven innocent or the culprit is found, you are relieved of your duties."

The brush slipped from her fingers. "You're firing me?" He couldn't do that. "Whatever happened to innocent until proven guilty? Don't you think the police would have arrested me if they believed I did what you are accusing me of?"

He turned his head away. "Leave now, Sierra. Don't make this any worse."

His eyes plead with her to understand, but she couldn't. It made no sense. She stomped past him. And to think she was once attracted to him. "You're wrong about me, John."

"I hope so. I don't want to believe you are capable of hurting my mom."

She whirled around. "Answer me this. If I wanted to hurt your mom, why would I risk my life to get her out of the house?"

He shrugged. "Hero complex? Maybe you never intended for her to get hurt. Saving her was a way to make you look innocent and draw attention away from the phone call you made."

She closed her eyes against the burning sensation behind them. "You're making a big mistake."

"Please leave."

She blinked away sudden tears and rushed from the room. She bumped into someone on the way out. "Excuse me." Her gazed collided with Celia's. Was that a smirk on her face?

"Are you okay?" Celia asked.

"I'm fine. What are you doing here? This wing is closed to guests."

"Oh. I didn't realize." She shrugged.

Yeah, right, and red doesn't mean stop. She needed to find Spencer.

John stared after Sierra. He wanted to follow her and tell her the truth, but knew this was for the best. At least he hoped it was. Spencer and Mark's plan better work. He hated to hurt Sierra, but they felt it would help draw the real bad guy out if they believed someone else was being blamed.

They would stop going after his family, or they would slip up and get caught. Spencer assured him he would keep a close eye on Sierra to make sure she was safe.

The look of disbelief and devastation on her face about did him in. If only he could have told her what was going on. But he'd promised to keep the plan to himself. Since they didn't know whom they could and couldn't trust, everyone, including Sierra, needed to believe she was a strong suspect in the arson.

CHAPTER NINETEEN

SIERRA'S PHONE RANG. SHE CHECKED THE caller I.D. and one corner of her lips turned up, in spite of her bad mood. "Hey, Spencer." She wrapped an arm around her waist as she pulled open the drapes in Mrs. Drake's house. Sunlight streamed in.

"Hey, yourself. Are you free for dinner tonight?"

"As a matter of fact, my schedule is completely open for the foreseeable future."

"Uh-oh. What happened?"

"John fired me yesterday."

"You're kidding? Are you sure he didn't just mean for you to lay low for a while?"

"No. He let me go."

"I'm sorry."

"Me too. I'd love to have dinner with you. Is this a date?"

"Yes. I thought I'd grill steaks."

"Delicious." This man had a way of making her feel good even when she was at her lowest. They firmed up their plans.

"Okay then, I'll see you tonight."

"Sounds good. 'Bye." She pocketed her phone then gazed out the window. A couple of deer munched on the foliage behind the house. They looked so peaceful as though they didn't have a care in the world—the same way she felt when with Spencer. She looked forward to their date tonight.

"Mom? What are you doing? Shouldn't you be at work?"

She turned to face her son. "Not today. I'm going to pack and get ready to move."

"It won't take that long to pack. Most of our stuff is in storage."

"I know, but I also want to thoroughly clean this place."

"Isn't Mrs. Drake paying someone to do that?"

"Yes. It's a girl thing. You wouldn't understand." Mrs. Drake might be paying someone to come in and clean, but she'd still leave the place spotless.

The day flew by and before she realized it, it was time to shower and get ready for her date. She'd already packed everything except for a pair of black capris and a red top as well as jeans and a T-shirt for tomorrow—moving day.

An hour later she stood at the door. "Call if you need anything, Trey. I'll be at Spencer's."

He rushed from his room. "Can I come?"

"Uh . . . it's kind of a . . . date."

He jerked his head back. "Oh. Well, say hi for me."

She rested her hand on the doorknob. "Are you okay with this?"

"Yeah. You were right. He's a good guy, once I got past the whole gun thing."

Relief washed over her. "I'm glad. Thanks, and next time you can come. Okay?"

He nodded. "What's for dinner?"

"There's a salad in the fridge and a box of mac and cheese on the counter."

"Cool. Thanks."

"Sure thing." Although the mac and cheese from a box fell short of being a nutritional meal, it was her son's favorite, and he liked to make it. "I shouldn't be too late."

He wore a dopey smile.

"What?"

"You're going on a date. I don't remember you ever doing that."

"That's because I don't date."

"No. You *didn't* date, but you do now. Have a good night, Mom."

"Thanks. You too." She walked out and locked up after herself. Her son would be a man soon. It would be good for him to have a role model like Spencer in his life. Not for the first time, she was glad she'd met him.

A short while later, she pulled up to his place and slid from her SUV. Spencer stood in the doorway with a dishtowel tossed over his shoulder. Her heart tripped. He looked good in dark jeans and a black T-shirt. She walked toward him. "Hi, there."

"Hi, yourself. Come on in. I put the steaks on a minute ago and am whipping up the salad dressing." He moved to the side, allowing her entrance.

"You make it from scratch?" She stepped inside his house.

"Don't you?" He raised a brow.

"Once in a while, I suppose. But it's not a normal thing." She breathed in deeply the yeast-scented air. "You baked bread too?"

"Not quite. I bought a loaf that only needed to be baked. I take short cuts when needed. I know my culinary limits."

She chuckled. "Are you enjoying your new kitchen?"

"Can't you tell?"

She looked around the small space and noted almost every countertop had something going on. Including a cheesecake on a cake stand. Yes, the man enjoyed the space. She had no idea he was such a foodie. "Would you like me to stack these dishes in the dishwasher?"

"Nope. I know it looks like a disaster, but it will only take a few minutes to clean this up. Most everything is on the grill outside."

"Ah, so you're a grill master."

"In my dreams." He rinsed the whisk then placed it into the dishwasher. "Everything is ready outside. I thought we could eat on the deck."

"Sounds good to me."

He pulled open the French doors they'd ended up installing during the remodel.

She gasped. "You re-did your outdoor space. It looks great!"

"Thanks. With as much time as I spend out here, I figured it was worth the extra investment. So you approve?"

She nodded. "Yes. You did a fine job." A teak loveseat, two chairs and coffee table rested atop an orange indoor/outdoor rug with a chevron pattern. "You really brought the indoors out." She looked around to see what else he'd done. The old patio table was missing—good. It had been an eyesore. She'd really wanted to do this space for him, but clearly he hadn't needed her help.

"Thanks. It wasn't difficult. I went down to a store in Bend and told them what I had in mind. They had this set up just like this, and I bought the display."

She laughed. "Whatever works."

"Have a seat while I check the potatoes. We're having mushroom Kabobs, roasted red potatoes, a cucumber and tomato salad—that's what the dressing was for, along with fresh bread, steak, and a strawberry cheesecake for dessert."

"Wow!" Good thing the waistband on her pants stretched. "That's a feast." Who was this man? His domestic side awed her. He was definitely a man of many talents.

Spencer transferred the food to a platter and placed it on the coffee table.

"Everything smells amazing."

"Let's hope it tastes that way too." He bowed his head and offered a quick blessing.

"How'd you know to pray?" She asked, looking stunned.

"I watch TV." He chuckled. "Plus you did when I've eaten with you, *and* the discipleship pastor at church is mentoring me. We meet once a week for coffee, and he always prays a blessing over our time together and the food or drink as the case may be."

"Hmm. I never had anyone in my life like that. You're really into this mentoring thing."

He took her plate and placed a juicy steak on it, then a skewer of mushrooms, a scoop of salad, then potatoes. "I suppose I see the value in it. Is that too much food?" Maybe he should have let her serve herself.

"It's perfect. Thanks. Should I go grab the bread?"

He knew he'd forgotten something. "Nope. I've got it. Be right back." He darted inside, grabbed the basket he'd placed it in then headed back outside. "Here you go."

"Thanks. I know I should avoid bread as it seems to go directly to my hips, but it smells divine."

"Your hips look perfect to me. I don't think a slice of bread will harm them."

Her cheeks pinked.

He chuckled. "Too forward?"

She held up her hand and pinched her finger together then pulled them a little apart. "A smidge."

"Sorry." He served up his plate then dug in. *Delicious.* He watched Sierra's face for her response. Pleasure shone. *Whew!* After all she'd been going through, he'd wanted to treat her to something special.

They ate in comfortable silence. She only ate half of what he'd served her then set her plate on the coffee table. "You're finished?"

"Yes. It was delicious, but I can't eat another bite."

"You hardly ate anything."

She chuckled. "I'm not a big person, Spencer. If I ate as much as you do, I'd be two sizes bigger."

"So no cheesecake?" Disappointment hit him. He should have let her serve herself.

She shot him a cheeky grin. "I saved room for dessert. When I said I couldn't eat another bite, it wasn't because I was full, but rather, I was satisfied."

The disappointment melted away and was replaced by admiration. Good for her. Now that he thought about it, he wasn't hungry any longer either. He placed his plate on the table as well. "I almost hate to bring it up because I don't want to upset you, but what are you going to do about a job?"

"I don't know. I'm in the process of buying a house here in Sunriver thinking we'd be here a good long while, but now . . ." She shrugged. "I'm taking one day at a time."

He nodded. "Sounds like a good idea for now. Are you still planning to move into my buddy's place tomorrow?"

"Yes. I can't wait to be out of Mrs. Drake's house. Don't get me wrong, it's an incredible home, but being there is no longer enjoyable."

"I understand. That was pretty rotten of her to do that to you and Trey."

"Exactly." Fire lit her eyes. "If it was only me affected by her actions, I wouldn't be so upset, but it affects my son too, and that does not set well."

He hurt for her, but knew of no way to make things better. "How about you come sit over here?" He patted the space beside him on the loveseat.

Her eyes widened and to his delight she stood and did exactly that. "This is even more comfortable than the chair, which I thought was quite comfy. You did well in buying this set."

"Thanks." He draped an arm across the back and rested his hand on her shoulder. "When I first met you, I never imagined us sitting here like this." Experience had taught him to take things slow when it came to women. He hoped the signals she was sending could be trusted. He'd been burned before and didn't care to go there again. But Sierra wasn't like that. She was easy to read, maybe too easy at times, but that wasn't necessarily a bad thing.

"Me neither." She chuckled. "I'd love to forget about

our first encounter."

"I think we all would. At least Trey seems to have gotten past it."

"Yes. I agree." She rested her head on his shoulder. "I could sit here like this all night, but I promised Trey I wouldn't be late. Let's go clean up, then have dessert."

"Sounds like a good plan." He stood and pulled her up with him. They stood so close he could feel her breath on his shoulder. He stepped back. Now was not a good time to kiss her silly. They might do something they'd both regret. And he didn't want any more regrets.

"I'll stop by tomorrow and accompany you and Trey over to my friend's place."

"That's not necessary."

"I want to. Besides, I have the key." He waggled his brows.

She laughed. "Okay. Just don't do that thing with your brows in front of Trey. He'll think you're weird."

"Aren't we all a little weird?" Pleasure shot through him—if only they could spend every evening like this bantering back and forth.

"Penny for your thoughts?" She looked up into his face.

"They're worth way more than that."

"Oh really? In that case . . ." She stood on tiptoe and placed a soft kiss on his cheek, then said softly, "I'll save up."

His heart tripped. She had an effect on him no other woman had ever had. He was in big trouble, if he was reading her signals wrong.

CHAPTER TWENTY

SIERRA HOISTED HER SUITCASE INTO HER SUV. "Do you have everything, Trey?"

"Yes. You okay, Mom?" He reached up and pulled the door closed. "You haven't been yourself for a couple of days."

How could she tell her son she'd lost her job? It wasn't fair. None of this was. She never should have given up their apartment and moved to Sunriver. For that matter, she never should have taken the job working for the Belafontes. She'd been doing fine before, even if it wasn't in her career field. At least at her former job, no one had accused her of things she hadn't done.

A hand touched her shoulder. She jumped, but it was only her son. "Trey. What do you need?"

"Something's wrong. I'm old enough to take it. Just tell me."

She sighed.

Spencer pulled up in his pickup, parked, then sauntered over to them. "You all moved out?"

She nodded. "I'm glad you're here." His friendship had meant so much these past few days. He was like a rock to her shifting sand life. She reached for his hand and gave it a gentle squeeze. "Do you have the key?"

"I do. I'll meet you there. I still want to check out the place. Make sure everything looks normal."

Her pulse surged. "Is that really necessary?"

"Probably not, but it would make me feel better." He released her hand and slipped an arm around her waist, then whispered into her ear. "It's going to be okay, Sierra. I promise." He placed a soft kiss on her temple.

She blinked away sudden tears. Trey couldn't see her lose it. She'd barely held herself together these past few days, and Spencer's tender kindness threatened to send her tumultuous emotions spiraling out of control. She cleared her throat. "We should get going."

Trey looked from her to Spencer. A knowing look filled his eyes. Good. Let him focus on her growing relationship with Spencer. She'd much rather deal with that than her current unemployment and arsonist suspect status.

She moved away from Spencer and sat behind the wheel. "Let's go, Trey." She put down the window.

Spencer rested a hand on the sill. "I'll follow. You know the way, right?"

"Yes. See you there." She waited for him to get into his pickup then backed out. Ever since the Belafonte family had turned their backs on her, Spencer had practically become her shadow. She didn't understand why—unless he thought she was guilty. She gasped.

"What?" Trey asked.

"I just thought of something." There was no way Spencer thought she was guilty. He wouldn't deceive her like that—then again, he was a man. Her track record with men wasn't great. But Spencer was different. He seemed genuine compared to other men who had tried to gain her affections over the years. Besides that, she really and truly liked him. She couldn't have the kind of feelings she had for him if he was deceiving her. Could she?

"Mom, what's wrong?"

"Nothing."

"You're lying, and you're freaking me out. I've tried to give you space like John and Spencer said to do, but—"

"Wait. John told you to give me space? When did you see him?" She glanced toward her son then quickly returned her focus to the road.

"I don't know. We run together. I guess last I saw him was a couple of days ago."

"I don't want you to run with him anymore."

"Why?" His voice hitched.

She sighed. "I really didn't want to have to tell you this, but I can see you need to know. John fired me."

"What happened?"

"It seems the Belafontes believe I started the fire at Mona's house."

"That's crazy. You'd never do anything like that. John didn't say anything to me. I can't believe he did that."

"Me either, until he fired me," she muttered. What kind of game was John playing? Whatever it was, he needed to leave her son out of it. "I don't trust John any more, and I would prefer if you don't run with him in the future."

Trey stared out the side window. "Okay."

Her mom-heart broke for her son. He'd looked up to John, and she could tell he was hurting. "Maybe once they find the real arsonist things will get better and you can run with him again." She tried to add a cheerful lilt to her voice, but it came out sounding forced.

"No. I don't want to run with him now."

Her throat burned. "I'm sorry, Trey." She glanced his

way.

He shrugged. "Don't worry about it. Spencer's cool. What I don't get, though, is if you're a suspect, why Spencer is being so . . . ah, friendly."

She chuckled. "You and me both, but I'm not complaining." It felt so weird talking to her son like this. But maybe it was a good thing. He was nearly grown and needed to have grownup conversations from time to time.

He laughed.

She gripped the steering wheel tighter. "What's so funny?"

"Spencer. I knew he had a thing for you from the first day he knocked on our door."

A tiny smile tugged at her mouth. "I suppose you could be right. But we're only friends."

"Friendly friends, too." He shot her a teasing grin, then pointed. "You're going to miss your turn."

"Ack!" She hit the brake hard, signaled and turned onto the cul-de-sac, parking at the first house.

Trey jumped out. She took a moment to collect herself. The driver's door flung open. Her gaze slammed into Spencer's.

"You going to sit there all day?" He held out his hand.

Her heart thundered. "Nope." She undid the seatbelt, took his hand, and walked beside him to the door. The small house reminded her a lot of the one she was buying. At least she hoped she was still buying it. What if the bank found out she'd lost her job?

Spencer unlocked the door and thrust it open. "Home sweet home." He turned to her. "Why don't you and Trey go grab your bags while I take a look around?"

Unease gripped her. Why did he think precaution was

necessary? It was time they had a talk. She needed to know what was really going on. She grabbed her bags then waited beside Trey for the all clear.

Spencer approached the door, smiling. "Welcome home."

Home. Kind of a relative term lately. "Thanks. After I put my suitcases in my room, can we talk?"

"Sure. It's a nice day. We could take a walk."

"I'd like that." She climbed the narrow stairs to the loft and dropped her suitcases beside one door. "How's the room, Trey?"

"It's fine. I have homework. Do you know the Wi-Fi password?"

"It's on a pad by the phone downstairs."

"Thanks." He shot past her with his laptop and trotted down the stairs.

She cringed as his shoulder rubbed against the rough, wood covered wall.

Spencer stood at the bottom of the stairwell. He offered his arm as she reached the last step. "Which direction should we go?"

"Doesn't matter to me," she said.

He led the way out the door. "We won't be too long, Trey," Spencer said as he closed and locked the door behind them. "So what's on your mind?"

"Too much."

He shot her a sympathetic grin. Her insides warmed. How she had ever been annoyed by him, she had no idea. He was really very sweet. "Maybe start with what prompted you to ask to talk."

"Right. I get the feeling you don't think I'm safe. What's up with that?"

"I'm a cop. Being cautious goes with the territory. It's nothing specifically to do with you."

"Honestly?"

"Yes. I won't lie to you, Sierra."

"I appreciate that. Then maybe you can tell me why John accused me of starting his mom's house on fire then fired me."

He winced before looking over his shoulder. "There is enough circumstantial evidence to make you appear guilty of all the stuff that has been going on."

"But I'm innocent. You know that. Why don't they believe in me too?"

Silence met her question.

What was he hiding? He'd said he wouldn't lie to her, but wasn't not telling her something every bit as bad? "Please, Spencer. I need to know what you're not saying."

He drew her over to a boulder situated between the paved path and the house and seated her beside him. "Against my better judgment, I will tell you as much as I think you need to know, but you must trust me with the rest. Can you do that?"

She nodded. "It seems I have little choice."

"And I'm sorry about that." His gaze took in all the land around them. He lowered his voice. "Mark and I believe someone wants you to take the fall for all that has been going on. We are hoping they will tip their hand when they find out the family turned against you and fired you."

"I don't understand. How would my getting fired draw them out?"

"Think about it. They would presume you'd be angry, maybe even enough to take revenge. We expect the person or persons to do something big soon. We also expect whatever they do will leave evidence that will point to you."

"How can someone hate me that much?"

Spencer draped his arm across her shoulder and drew her against his side. "I doubt any of this has to do with you, but rather the convenience you provide. The family, their homes, and worksites are all under twenty-four-hour surveillance. Whoever is doing this will be caught."

"Wow. That must be expensive."

He didn't reply.

"So why are you with me and not on the surveillance crew?"

"My job is to give you an alibi. John's request."

"Oh." He was only with her to provide an alibi, not because he wanted to be.

"Why do I feel like I said something wrong?"

"It's nothing."

"Yes, it's something and it's big. Please tell me."

She took a breath. "I was hoping you were with me because you wanted to be, not because you had to be."

He drew her close. "Aw, sweetie. I'm sorry you misunderstood. I volunteered because I *want* to be with you. I *need* to make sure you are safe and no one can hurt you. I don't think you realize how much I care for you."

She blinked back sudden tears and rested her head on his shoulder. "You are the kindest man I've ever known." The anger she'd harbored toward him dissipated. Relief flowed through her—she'd been right about him after all. "Oh." She sat up and twisted to face him. "Does that mean my job loss is only temporary?"

He shrugged. "I don't know. I wasn't supposed to tell

you about any of this. We felt like it would be easier if you didn't know, but I could see what not knowing was doing to you, and I can't stand seeing you hurt like that." He ran the back of his hand down her cheek. "I won't let anyone hurt you."

"I know you won't." She looked into his eyes, wishing he wasn't such a gentleman. She wanted him to kiss her more than anything right now. She looked away before she kissed him and embarrassed herself.

Spencer's heart hammered as he gently turned Sierra's face toward his. The gold flecks in her eyes darkened. "May I kiss you?"

She nodded.

His lips met hers. She slid an arm around his neck deepening the kiss before pulling back. A twinkle lit her eyes. "I was hoping you'd do that."

"Oh, yeah? Then you won't mind if I do it again." He loved her. Pure and simple. He hadn't realized until this moment the depth of his feelings.

She placed a soft peck on his lips, then slid off the boulder. "How about that walk?"

"Or we could sit here and make out." He flicked a grin.

She laughed. "I don't think so. My son is an impressionable teenage boy, and I'm pretty sure that I just spotted the curtains in the house move."

He chuckled. "Okay. You win."

A police vehicle pulled up behind Sierra's car. "That's

odd. I wonder why Mark is here."

Mark stepped out and approached them. A grim look covered his face.

Spencer's gut tightened.

Sierra grasped his arm. "Were you expecting Mark?"

"No." He stood and waited in place for Mark. "What's going on?"

"I have a warrant for Sierra's arrest."

He stepped in front of her. "What are you talking about? All the evidence against her is circumstantial."

"Captain's orders. I'm sorry, Sierra."

"Spencer, you can't let him arrest me. I thought the police were on my side." Panic filled her voice.

His chest tightened and pain gripped him. "I'll get to the bottom of this. Don't worry." He took her hand and gave it a gentle squeeze.

"What about Trey?"

"I'll take care of him. Don't worry. Everything will be okay."

"I don't see how." Her voice caught.

Trey stepped outside. "What's going on?" He jogged over to them.

Thankfully Mark hadn't put cuffs on Sierra. "Your mom is being arrested for starting the fire at Mona Belafonte's house."

"She didn't do that!" He looked to Sierra. "Mom, tell them."

"They know, honey. You stay with Spencer, and I'll get home as soon as I can." She shot Spencer a look—fear filled her eyes, but so did strength.

CHAPTER TWENTY-ONE

SIERRA SAT IN A ROOM AT the police department. When would an officer come in and talk to her? She'd already been processed, but rather than put her in a cell, a female officer had brought her to this room and left her. Was this some sort of torture tactic? Leave her long enough, she'd confess to a crime she didn't commit?

She refused to believe things were as bad as they appeared. She trusted the justice system. Something must be keeping them. Maybe they'd caught the real bad guy—that had to be it.

The door finally opened and Mark walked in.

She breathed a little easier. Mark was a good guy, and she trusted him for the most part—at least she had until he'd arrested her. But she couldn't hold that against him. He was only doing his job. "Is my son okay?"

"Yes. This conversation is being recorded. Please tell me about the fire at Mona's house."

She frowned. "I've already given my statement." Why was he being so formal with her? He'd been one of her dinner guests not all that long ago, and now he talked as though he was a stranger. She pressed her lips together. "Why am I here?"

"A witness spotted you at the scene."

"Excuse me? What are you talking about? I was in Bend. John can tell you that." Although he might not be willing to, all things considered. How did this happen? Who would lie? "Mark, you know as well as I do that I'm being set up. There is no way I can be two places at once."

"I'm following orders, Sierra. According to the timeline you did have time to set that fire, and in light of the witness account, things have changed."

What was that supposed to mean? Had everyone turned against her? "I want a lawyer."

"That's your right." He slid a piece of paper across the table to her. "Spencer asked me to have you sign this. It gives him guardianship of your son until all of this gets cleared up."

She took the paper and scanned it, not missing the hopeful words Mark had spoken. He believed this would get cleared up. She should be relieved, but she wasn't. This could ruin her. She didn't have a lot of money to begin with. Now she had to pay an attorney. There was always the option of a public defender, but from what she'd heard they were overworked and underpaid and wouldn't have time to devote to her case.

She signed the paper and placed the pen beside it. "Now what?"

"You wait for your arraignment."

"Can I see Spencer?"

He shook his head. "No." Regret filled his eyes.

Fear gripped her. Why was this happening, and why wouldn't they let her see Spencer?

"You need to stay away from Sierra Robbins," Captain

Michaels said. "I don't want there to be any hint of impropriety that could compromise this case."

Spencer drew in a breath and let it out in a whoosh. He stood before the captain. "Assuming she signs the form I sent in with Mark, I will be Sierra's son's legal guardian. I'm as entangled in her life as a person can get, sir."

Captain Michaels nodded. "Agreed. You haven't had a real vacation since you've been here. I checked with human resources and noted you have a lot of vacation time accumulated."

"Good point. Does that mean I can cash in some time?" He wondered at the captain's suggestion, but considering all that was going on, it was a good idea to step away from work for a while.

"Yes. I have a feeling things here are going to get worse before they improve, and the farther away you are, the better."

"What do you know that I don't?"

"The media picked up the story, and it's going nationwide."

He groaned and nearly cursed before stopping himself. This was bad, very bad. Now he understood Captain Michaels' caution. "Okay. I'll let HR know I'm taking a vacation until this case is wrapped up."

"Thank you. I'll make sure your shifts are covered. You'd better get out of here. There's a press conference scheduled in an hour."

"What's the deal with the press? This isn't a huge story."

"Someone made it a big deal."

"Who?"

"Our witness."

Spencer raised a brow hoping for a name, but Captain Michaels pressed his lips together. Fine. He'd find out on his own. "See you." He left without a backward glance.

It was time to enlist those prayer warriors he'd heard about at church. But first, he'd try to sneak in a quick visit with Sierra before she was moved. He had to make sure she was okay. He slipped down the hall and knocked once before entering. Empty.

"She's gone, buddy."

Spencer turned and faced Mark. "I was hoping to see her."

Mark thrust a paper at him. "She signed." He looked over his shoulder and lowered his voice. "Between you and me, I'm still on her side. I'll be looking into the witness."

"Good. Thanks." He rubbed the back of his neck and looked from side to side. "I suppose I should get out of here before this media frenzy I heard about appears."

"Yeah. A few reporters have already set up out there."

"Great. Good thing I'm not in uniform. I'll see you around." He walked as casually as possible through the parking lot to his pickup, noting two camera crews were already in place for the press conference. Thankfully, they didn't know his connection to the case.

He headed to his buddy's house to pick up Trey. No way was he leaving the teen alone there. He'd bring him to his place where he could protect him from the media. At least they had no idea where Sierra had been planning to stay.

He drove up to the cabin and used the extra key his buddy had given him to let himself inside. "Trey! It's me, Spencer. Pack up. You're coming to my place. Grab your mom's bags, too."

Trey charged down the stairs. He looked around the room. "Where is she? I thought you'd bail her out and bring her back with you."

"She has to be arraigned first. I'm sorry. We need to clear out. Do you want help with the suitcases?" The disappointment on Trey's face tore him in two. He'd do anything for this kid, but he had to follow the law. He couldn't break Sierra out. This wasn't a movie.

"Yeah. Mom has two. They're in her room."

He followed the teen up the stairs to the loft. Moving from place to place had to be difficult. He determined to provide a stable home for Trey until his mom could resume that task. He had to believe that wouldn't be too long from now, but unease settled in the recesses of his mind. What if she was wrongly convicted on the testimony of one person and circumstantial evidence? It wouldn't be the first time that had happened.

He had to figure out who was behind all the trouble.

John hammered the nail into a board at his mother's house. Thankfully, only the backside of the house needed to be repaired. The smoke damage inside was another matter. He still struggled to grasp that Sierra had done this—she'd been with him not long before she got to the house. How could she possibly have had time to set the fire and for it to become so fully engaged so quickly? Then again, gasoline is quite the accelerant. His gut said she didn't do this, yet the police had an eyewitness.

"There's another reporter here, John. Will you go and deal with him?" Rick came through the back door and motioned outside.

John sighed. He'd been elected the spokesman for the family—not an election he wished to win. He set his tool belt aside and headed toward the front of his mother's house. A reporter stood in the driveway wearing a dark business suit.

The reporter waved. "Thanks for agreeing to talk with me."

"No problem." John looked around for a cameraperson, but spotted no one. "You travel light. Most of the reporters who come here bring along a photographer at the very least."

The man shrugged and offered his hand. "I do it all." He held out his hand. "I'm Randy."

"I'm John Belafonte. What can I do for you?" The man stood at about six feet tall, had clean-cut hair, and he was an older version of Trey. How crazy was that?

"I'd like to ask you a few questions about the woman the police arrested. I understand she worked for your family."

"Correct."

"The other media outlets have covered your family and the crime, but no one has dug deeply into the suspect."

John crossed his arms and narrowed his eyes.

Randy adjusted his tie as if it was strangling him. "I understand that Sierra has a son? With his mom locked up, is he in state custody or what?"

"What paper did you say you are with?"

Randy cleared his throat and mumbled something

incoherent.

"I can't help you, buddy." He noted the silver Taurus with California plates in the driveway that clearly belonged to the man. "I suggest you leave. Maybe the police can assist you."

"Come on. I drove a long way for a scoop. Help a guy out."

"I don't think so. You're on private property. It's time for you to leave—now." His voice had turned to steel. If this dude knew what was good for him, he'd leave before John delivered the police to him. The man had to be Trey's dad. He must have seen the media coverage about Sierra. But why show up after all these years when he'd given up custody?

"Everything okay?" Rick asked as he rounded the house.

"Randy here was just leaving."

The man's gaze moved from John to his brother. "Look, I just want to know about the kid."

Rick marched up to them. "Seems to me you've overstayed your welcome. The police drop by on a regular basis, and we are under surveillance at all times." He pointed to a video camera pointing in their direction attached to the front porch.

Randy's face blanched. He spun around and strode to his car.

Rick turned to John. "You get his license plate number?"

John tapped his head. "I'll give Mark a call and let him know. I can't say for certain, but I'm pretty sure that was Trey's dad."

Sierra sat in her cell staring at the wall. Her attorney said he'd get her out soon, but she'd been in here four days! What was going on? She'd had her arraignment and bail had been set. Why was it taking so long to bail her out, and why hadn't anyone come to see her to let her know? Her attorney had been incognito since she'd met him that first day. Maybe she should find a new one.

She'd tried to remain strong, but she couldn't take much more of this place. Her body trembled constantly. She'd probably aged ten years since being arrested. And worst of all, she hadn't been able to see Trey. She couldn't imagine what he was going through. She was all he had. He must be terrified. She had to get out and soon. Her son needed her.

Lord, I don't understand why you allowed all of this to happen. I'm scared and I'm angry. Super angry. It's not fair that I'm locked up in here when the real arsonist is free.

I am with you. Do not fear.

Easier said than done. She never wanted to see the inside of a jail cell again. Moving around from home to home didn't even matter—she saw things with a new perspective now. They'd had a warm and comfortable place to sleep and call home, even if it was temporary.

The first thing she was going to do when she got out of here was take a shower then hold onto her son and not let go. Surely the police would figure out they had the wrong person and set her free. But what if they didn't?

Voices drew her attention. She sat up straight and watched through the bars to see who approached.

Her cell door slid open. She stood. "Does this mean my bail was paid, and I can leave?"

The female guard nodded. "You'll be escorted to a waiting vehicle."

"Why? Is that normal?"

"You have received several death threats."

Tears burned her eyes. "Someone wants me dead?" Her voice sounded like a little child's. "Why?" She thought going to jail was the worst thing that could happen to her, but a death threat felt much worse. She had no idea how she managed to stay standing on her rubbery legs.

They made their way through security then the guard guided her to a non-public door and pushed it open. Another guard stood there apparently waiting for them.

Fear overcame Sierra as she walked between the two guards to a waiting black SUV with tinted windows. She wiped tears from her face with the back of her hands.

One officer opened the door and she scooted inside. The door closed. She didn't recognize the man behind the wheel. "Where are you taking me?"

"I'm a friend of Spencer's. He's asked me to make sure no one follows us, so we'll be taking a roundabout way to his place. He asked me to tell you that Trey is with him, and he's fine."

Praise God. She let her breath out in a long sigh, rested her head back, and closed her eyes. "Thanks." A sob escaped. She fought to gain control of her emotions. She was finally free and Spencer was waiting for her with Trey.

A moment later her lids shot open. "What if someone does follow us or tries to run us off the road, or crashes into us?"

His brown eyes met her gaze in the reflection of the

rearview mirror. "Relax, Sierra. I'm a federal agent. Trained to deal with this sort of thing. You're safe."

Spencer had a friend in the FBI? Why not? Nothing should surprise her at this point. "Thanks for taking care of me. So the threat is credible?"

"Yes."

"I wish I understood why someone is so determined to either destroy me or kill me."

"There are some good people working to find that out."

"I had no idea. Does this threat have anything to do with my extended stay in jail?"

"Yes. Spencer had to work out the details to keep you and your son safe. Trey's dad came snooping around looking for him."

She leaned forward. "Randy was here?" Anger burned that he'd chose now to step up and be a dad, but surprise filled her as well.

"According to Spencer, yes. But he said everything is under control and that you are not to worry."

Again, easier said than done. But she truly trusted Spencer and the Lord. She took a few cleansing breaths and let the anger go. God was in control and clearly He was using Spencer and his friends to help her. For possibly the first time in her life she felt absolute peace. It seemed impossible, but here she was with the unwavering belief that everything was going to be okay.

Her eyes grew heavy and slid closed.

CHAPTER TWENTY-TWO

SPENCER PULLED OPEN THE BACK DOOR to Ben's SUV. Sierra sat there sound asleep. He touched her shoulder. "Sweetie. It's time to wake up."

She stretched. Her eyes fluttered open. She tilted her head and met his gaze. A smile tipped her lips. "Hi."

"Hi, yourself. You ready to go in?"

She unbuckled. "Thanks for the ride. I never did catch your name."

"Ben."

She nodded. "Thanks, Ben." She scooted to the door and slid out.

"Let's get you inside out of view of possible prying eyes."

She rushed into Spencer's home and immediately noted all the blinds were closed.

"Mom!" Trey rushed toward her and wrapped his arms around her. "I'm so glad you're here."

Sudden tears flowed. "Me too." She hugged him and took in the minty scent of his hair. "How's school going?"

He released his hold on her and stepped back. "I've been busy. So I'm a little behind."

She raised a brow. "Busy doing what?"

"Helping Spencer and stuff." He shrugged a shoulder.

"And stuff, huh? I suppose just this once I'll let it slide." She spotted Spencer watching them from his kitchen.

"You hungry, Sierra?" Spencer asked.

"Now that you mention it, I could eat, but first I'd love a shower."

"Your luggage is in the guestroom in the loft. Make yourself at home."

"Thanks." She retreated to the bathroom and took the much-needed shower. Afterward she slipped into leggings and a tunic. She only towel-dried her hair and skipped makeup. She had some catching up to do now that she felt more like herself.

One thing had nagged at her since she'd been delivered here. She went out to the main living area and spotted Spencer, Ben, and Trey gathered around the kitchen counter talking. It was on the tip of her tongue to ask why they were at his place when a knock sounded on the door.

Spencer pulled out his sidearm and motioned them into the bedroom down the hall.

She grabbed Trey's hand and together they fled. She closed the door but stayed close, hoping to hear what was going on.

"I need to tell you something."

She knew that voice. Celia? Sierra pulled the door open. Trey grabbed her arm. She shrugged him off. "It's okay. I know her."

"She could be the bad guy, Mom," he whispered.

He had a point. She'd wait until Spencer said it was okay to come out. She turned and took in the room she hadn't seen when she'd drawn up the design for his remodel. Since her job had focused on the kitchen, master suite, and loft there was no reason to come in this room.

Though there was nothing fancy about it, it was homey with two single beds pushed against opposite walls. A nightstand sat between the beds with plenty of space between it and the beds.

A desk that her son had obviously been using was situated on the same wall as the door. She pulled out the chair and sat. What was taking Spencer so long?

About twenty minutes later a knock sounded on the door. "Sierra, you can come out now."

Ben stood in the entryway and Celia sat on the couch. Her eyes looked red as if she'd been crying.

"What's going on," she whispered to Spencer.

"Celia has something she'd like to tell you." He took her hand and gave it a gentle squeeze. "It's okay. She's unarmed and poses no threat to you—in fact, just the opposite."

Sierra sat across from Celia. "I hear you want to talk with me."

Celia nodded. "I have a story for you, and I hope you won't be angry with me, but I'll understand if you are."

Sierra looked to Spencer who stood beside Ben talking in low tones she couldn't hear.

"As you know, Mrs. Drake is my godmother."

Sierra nodded.

"Well, she has a brother. His name is Carl Davis. Carl and the Belafontes go way back. Mr. Belafonte and Carl were competitors in the construction business, but Carl wasn't a good businessman and had a difficult time managing money. From what I understand, Mr. Belafonte kept undercutting Carl's bids and getting the jobs he wanted. It got to be so bad that Carl closed his business and declared bankruptcy."

Sierra's eyes widened. "Carl is the man who works for Mrs. Drake. I met him the day I moved in."

"Yes. That's correct."

"This is all interesting, but where is this story going, and why are you the one sharing it?"

Sadness filled Celia's eyes. "I'm here because what they did was wrong. I read about everything in the paper. I'm so sorry. It's all my fault. I let jealousy blind me to what they were doing."

"What do you mean?"

"My godmother was very curious about you and what you were doing while you were living in her house, so I would report to her. She wanted more and more information, like where you were working, so I resorted to following you sometimes. I knew the history her brother had with the Belafontes, but my godmother always laughed off his attitude. She never seemed to care one way or the other about the family and even rooted for me when I was invited to interview to be Bailey's assistant. But when I didn't get the job, things changed."

Sierra couldn't believe what she was hearing, but it all made sense somehow.

"I was angry and hurt that you were chosen over me. You see, I remembered you from school, and I knew I was a better designer than you. I didn't realize it at the time, but my godmother decided to wage war against you and the Belafontes when I didn't get the job." Her tearful gaze slammed into Sierra's. "You have to believe me. I didn't realize what she and her brother were doing. By the time I did, you were in jail and the media circus had begun. Carl started that fire . . . I knew something had to be done before someone was killed."

"I don't understand. How could you not have known what they were up to?"

Celia sighed. "I believed my godmother had left the country. She was in reality staying at a motel in Bend where she and her brother schemed to destroy the Belafontes. The fire was never intended to kill Mona. Carl was counting on you getting there before it was too late—"

"Hold on. He was willing to risk an elderly woman's life because of a grudge? That's insane."

"No, that's hate," Spencer said. "Celia went to the police and already gave her statement. Mark told her where you were, so she could explain everything in person. Although I wish he would have run it by me first, but that's another conversation."

"You really knew nothing?" Sierra asked.

Celia shook her head. "Not until after the fire did I put it all together. I was afraid. I love my godmother as if she were my own mom, but what they did to you was wrong. They set you up because of me. She was angry that you got the job, and I didn't. I'm so sorry for everything. Seeing what they did opened my eyes to my own role in their hate. I'm really sorry."

Sierra sat silent, too numb to reply.

"You were nice to me," Celia said. "Even when I was a snot. And I respected your honest sass at the shop. When I read everything in the paper and that you could spend serious jail time, I knew I had to come forward."

If Spencer and Ben hadn't been standing there affirming what Celia said she wouldn't have believed her—this was crazy. Her life had turned into a soap opera. Thankfully it would be over soon. "Thank you, Celia. I'm sure it wasn't easy to turn them in."

"It was one of the hardest things I've ever done, but it felt good to free you. I'm only sorry it took me so long to figure out what was going on, and that I didn't turn them in immediately."

Spencer's phone rang. He spoke quietly then slipped the phone into his pocket. "All charges have been dropped."

"Woo-hoo!" Trey shouted from somewhere behind her.

They all laughed, releasing the heavy tension in the room. She was a free woman once again. Jobless, but free.

A knock sounded on Spencer's door. The men glanced at one another then Spencer looked out the peephole. He pulled the door partway open. "May I help you?"

"I'm looking for my son, Trey Robbins. Is he here?"

Sierra's heart beat a rapid staccato. Randy? She stood as Trey darted past her.

"Why would you think he's here?" Spencer asked

Ben moved to block her son.

"Let him go," Sierra said.

Trey tapped Spencer's shoulder. "I want to see him."

He flicked a glance over his shoulder and stepped aside. Sierra stood and moved closer. She hovered behind Spencer, close enough to hear what was going on, on the other side of the partly closed door.

"I got your message," Randy said.

"Thanks for coming. Everything is okay now. All the charges against my mom were dropped."

Trey had reached out to his dad? Her stomach churned. Had something happened with Spencer?

"I heard on the radio as I was driving over here from my hotel. I'm glad everything turned out for you and your mom."

"Me too. I'm sorry coming here was a bother."

"Are you kidding? You will never be a bother."

"That's not the way I understand things. You left and you gave up all your parental rights."

"You speak your mind. Good. That makes it easier. Yes. I did those things, but I was young and stupid. I'm not that kid anymore. I've grown into a man. I have a wife and kids, and I'd like you to meet them. They came with me to Oregon."

"Really?" Trey's voice hitched. "I have half-siblings?" He poked his head around the corner of the door. "Mom! You need to get out here."

Spencer gently squeezed her shoulder. "I'm here if you need me," he said softly. He pulled the door open wider and let her out.

She tugged it closed behind her. "It's been a while, Randy."

"Yes. I'm sorry about that."

She shrugged. "Why are you here now?"

"Our son found me and contacted me." His focus shifted to Trey. "By the way, how did you find me? I've thought to look for you and your mom over the years, but I didn't know where to start. She'd left our hometown and no one knew where she'd gone."

"My mom's boyfriend found you for us. He's a cop."

Randy chuckled. "Talk about irony. I saw the write-ups in the paper. I'm glad they found the persons responsible."

"Me too!" Trey said. "I was freaked out when my mom was arrested. That's the only reason I called you. I didn't want you in my life since you'd tossed me aside without a second thought."

Sierra studied the changing emotions crossing Randy's face as her son reamed him. She ought to remind him to talk respectfully, but she couldn't. Randy needed to hear this.

"What about now?" Randy asked.

"I don't know. Things have been so crazy. Thanks for dropping everything and coming."

"You weren't easy to find. You forgot to tell me where you were staying, and when I tried to call the number back, it always went to voicemail."

"I used a throw away phone."

"You didn't trust me?"

"I don't know you."

"But you called anyway."

"True."

"Randy, there's a lot going on right now," Sierra said. "If you're going to be around maybe you and Trey can meet for pizza. You can catch up, maybe exchange contact information, then you and your family can head back to California."

He nodded. "What do you say, Trey?"

"I guess so." He looked at her. "This is weird."

She laughed. "I agree. Meet us at the pizza place in the village tomorrow at six." She didn't wait for his reply and turned to go inside. She felt Trey right behind her.

Spencer stood with a grim look on his face. "Well?"

Ben cleared his throat. "That's my cue to leave. Celia, are you coming?"

"Ah, sure." She stood and stopped when she reached Sierra. "I'm glad you're okay, and I'm really sorry about everything."

"Thanks, Celia." Too many emotions clogged her mind at the moment. Talk about being in overload.

Ben and Celia walked out together leaving the three of them alone. They stood there in silence, until Trey moved to the couch.

"Are you mad at me, Mom?"

"Because you called your dad? No. I'm surprised, but not angry. I wish you'd let Spencer or myself know he might show up, though." She went and snuggled into the corner of the couch.

Trey sat across from her. "Yeah. I'm sorry about that too. I really didn't think he'd come. When we spoke on the phone, he was pretty weirded out."

"I would imagine so."

The couch shifted as Spencer eased down beside her. "So are you my girlfriend now?" He reached for her hand.

Tingles shot through her fingers and up her arms. "You heard that, huh?"

He nodded. Vulnerability shone in his eyes.

"I'd like to be your girlfriend." She'd finally found a man she could trust—one that wouldn't walk out on her when things got tough. He'd more than proven himself.

"Good. Because I have big plans for us."

Trey stood. "I'm leaving before things get gross."

They chuckled.

He stepped past them, and a moment later she heard the click of his bedroom door.

"Alone at last," Spencer said. "I've missed you." He tugged her closer and dropped feather-light kisses on her neck before moving to her face and ending on her lips. She returned his kiss and warmed from head to toe. This was what true love felt like.

EPILOGUE

SIERRA STOOD OUT ON THE DECK looking for her husband. Where had Spencer gone? Too many bodies filtered around their small house and yard to celebrate Trey's graduation from the University of Oregon. He'd studied to be an engineer like his dad.

"Spencer!" She stood on tiptoe and waved.

He made his way to her and pulled her to his side. "This is quite a turnout. I didn't think everyone on the guest list would show up at the same time."

She laughed. "Me either. Look, there's John and Sarah. Let's say hi." They wove their way through clumps of Trey's college friends and a few of their own as well. "You made it." She gave them each a quick hug.

John looked past them. "Looks like we choose a popular time to come."

Spencer pointed to the kitchen counter. "Help yourself to food and dessert while it's still there. Where are your kids?"

Sarah grinned. "Are you kidding? We wouldn't dream of bringing the twins to something like this. Imagine two active four-years-olds racing through your house." She shook her head. "I value your friendship too much to do that." A twinkle lit her eyes.

"You'll have to bring them each a piece of cake," Sierra said. "There are plates on the counter. Trey is outside."

Their friends moved further into the house. "I'm glad they came," she said.

"I'm glad they left their rascals at home." He chuckled and winked.

Sarah wasn't kidding about the energy level of their twins. The boys were a handful-and-a-half, but John and Sarah were great parents and the kids more than likely would have done fine. They probably wanted a break, and she didn't blame them.

The door swung open, and Bailey along with Stephen and their crew of three boys sauntered inside. Poor Bailey had wanted a girl so much, but had given up after having all boys.

Stephen offered his hand to Spencer. "Long time no see."

"No kidding. How've you been?" The men wandered off.

"Thanks for coming, Bailey."

"We wouldn't miss this. Where is the man of the hour?"

"Outside with his friends. Have some food and mingle. We invited the entire Belafonte clan, so I know there will be people here you know."

Bailey grinned. "How's business going?"

"Great." When Mrs. Drake went to prison for her role in the arson she'd lost her business. Sierra was able to purchase the inventory for pennies on the dollar. She'd given the space her own touch and had been taking on designing clients on the side.

Trey sidled up to her. "Mom, Randy is out front. I'm going to go out and say hi and invite him in." He had never felt comfortable calling Randy "Dad," but they had developed a decent relationship for which she was grateful. Her son had flourished under the care of Spencer and the attention of Randy. She couldn't ask for more.

She looked around the space and caught her husband's eye. Peace washed through her. Their love story had a rocky start, but their love had been designed by the Lord, and she couldn't be happier.

A Note from the Author

This is the final book in the Sunriver Dreams series. Thank you for coming on this journey with me. Sunriver is a favorite place of mine, and I hope you have grown to love it as much as I do.

I enjoy connecting with readers via my Kimberly Rose Johnson Reader's group on Facebook. If that's not your style, please subscribe to my newsletter via my website. www.kimberlyrjohnson.com

Books by Kimberly Rose Johnson

Sunriver Dreams
A Love to Treasure
A Christmas Homecoming
Designing Love

Wildflower B&B Romance Series
Island Refuge
Island Dreams
Island Christmas
Island Hope

Stand Alone
A Valentine for Kayla

Series with Heartsong Presents
The Christmas Promise
A Romance Rekindled
A Holiday Proposal
A Match for Meghan

70690334R00115

Made in the USA
Middletown, DE
16 April 2018